THE SUMMERBOY

A CHARLOTTE ZOLOTOW BOOK

THE SUMMERBOY

A NOVEL BY

ROBERT LIPSYTE

1 8 🏴 1 7

——— HARPER & ROW, PUBLISHERS ———

Cambridge, Philadelphia, San Francisco, London, Mexico City, São Paulo, Sydney

——— NEW YORK ———

The Summerboy

First Edition

Library of Congress Cataloging in Publication Data
Lipsyte, Robert.
   The summerboy.

   "A Charlotte Zolotow book."
   Summary: When Bobby Marks takes a summer job in a
laundry, he gets more than he bargains for: prejudice,
unrequited love, and other hazards.
   [1. Summer employment—Fiction] I. Title.
PZ7.L67Su 1982   [Fic]   82-47578
ISBN 0-06-023888-7   AACR2
ISBN 0-06-023889-5 (lib. bdg.)

For my parents,
Fanny and Sidney Lipsyte,
and for my sister,
Gale

1

I was tooling through the village of Rumson Lake on the day after my last final exam when I spotted the sign outside the Lenape Laundry:

**TRUCK HELPER WANTED
INQUIRE WITHIN**

I began to imagine myself behind the wheel of one of those big white delivery trucks with the familiar outline of a Lenape Indian chief on its sides. The really cool drivers steered standing up so they could lean out the door and call to girls along their route. In a white uniform with an Indian head on my back, a toothpick in my mouth, and a red Lenape baseball cap pulled low over my eyes, there was no way I wouldn't make out like a bandit.

The Lenape Laundry looked deserted as I swung my father's black Dodge, the Squaremobile, into the asphalt yard. I lost some of my confidence. The shades were drawn on the high, dusty windows of the massive white cinder-block building. Add barbed wire and a few gun turrets, it could pass for the state pen.

I might have driven right out again if I hadn't noticed

a little tan MG convertible parked alongside one of the trucks. Classy British sports cars were rare around Rumson Lake in 1956, and this one was a genuine chippie chaser. I got out of the Squaremobile for a closer look.

The steering wheel was on the right-hand side, British style. The instrument panel belonged in a Piper Cub. Chocolate-brown leather seats. A tan plaid cap hung rakishly from the knob of the floor shift. Very tweedy.

"Laundry's closed." A man stood in the side doorway marked EMPLOYEES ONLY. "Or did you come to steal the car?"

I thought fast. "I'm inquiring about the job."

His bright-blue eyes flicked over my college T-shirt, my chino pants, and my dirty white bucks. "The Laundry only hires all-year-rounders."

I didn't appreciate his snotty tone. "It's your loss," I said.

"Is it now?" His voice was sardonic.

I gave him the once-over. Tall, lean, sandy haired. Maybe thirty years old. He was wearing rumpled blue cord pants and a long-sleeved white shirt with a buttoned-down collar. A black knit tie hung at half-mast. He obviously belonged to the Tweedmobile. I figured him for a graduate student or a local high school English teacher making extra money as a weekend watchman. I could speak his language. But before I could think of anything to say, he said, "Come inside and amuse me."

I followed him through a dim passageway. I smelled bleach and soap. It was too dark to see more than the sharp outlines of machines in the huge main room of the plant.

He opened a frosted-glass door and ushered me into a little office. A fan was humming in a corner, stirring stale air. He sat down in a wooden swivel chair and propped his scuffed cordovan shoes on a wooden desk littered with books, typewritten papers, index cards, pens, an open thermos bottle, and half of a bologna sandwich. It reminded me of the cubbyhole office of my freshman adviser.

"Welcome to the sanctum sanctorum, hideout from worldly woes, wife, and child." He caught me peeking at his books. "Tell me what you know about the epic hero as outsider in western literature."

"I just did a term paper for English comparing Beowulf with contemporary antiheroes."

"Did you?" He smiled. He had little crinkles around his blue eyes. Except for his teeth, which were crooked, he was very handsome. "Which antiheroes?"

"I took Shane, the Humphrey Bogart character in *Casablanca*, and William Holden in *Stalag 17*, and . . ."

"Hollywood movies!" He wrinkled his nose. "If it was that easy I would have finished my thesis years ago."

I felt a little deflated. "What's your thesis?"

"I'm beginning to wonder myself." He lifted the thermos to his lips. From the way he swished the liquid around in his mouth before he swallowed and sighed, I guessed it wasn't lemonade. "What's your name?"

"Bob Marks."

"How old are you?"

"Eighteen."

He set down his thermos and studied me. "So. Why do you want to ride a laundry truck?"

"The same old story. Love and glory." It was from the big song in *Casablanca*.

He laughed, but I could tell he didn't recognize the words. Must be one of those ivory tower intellectual types who hates movies. I decided I liked him anyway. I didn't mind amusing him. He took another slug from his thermos.

"Unfortunately, Bob Marks, you'd be wasting your time applying. This is a real job, not a summer job. Moreover, the truck foreman here in hick heaven, a Neanderthal named Bump Ennis, believes that summer residents, in his quaint argot, ain't worth squat."

"What's his problem?"

He shrugged. "Who can fathom the native mind? Bump believes that summer residents are sunshine patriots, no roots in Lenape County, no local loyalty."

"Maybe I should set him straight."

"Doubtful. Bump even considers the current owner of the Laundry, Roger Sinclair, a summerboy."

Suddenly I wanted the job. Not only would I make out like a bandit, I'd show this Bump Ennis what a summerboy could do. Then I'd ride off, like Shane.

"On the other hand, Bob Marks, maybe you should work here. Give me a chuckle now and then." He swung his long legs off the desk and sat up. "You could tell Bump you ran out of money and quit college. Tell him you've got asthma—that way he won't think you'll be drafted as soon as he's trained you."

"I wouldn't want to start out by lying . . ."

"Silence! I'm thinking." He fished a blue pack of cigarettes out of his shirt pocket. "How do we convince Bump that a bright fellow like you would want to join this dismal swamp of demented greasers, drabs, harridans, cockeyed wenches, and hayseed bar brawlers?"

I wasn't exactly thrilled by the way he described the people who worked in the laundry, but I could understand how a frustrated doctoral student could spill out his bitterness for having to work here. So I let it pass. Besides, I was getting excited by the possibility of actually getting on a laundry truck.

"I could say that I want to be a writer, which is true, and that . . ."

". . . that a writer needs to observe real people at real work to get details for his novels."

"How'd you know?" I asked.

He lit his cigarette, took a long drag, and squinted at the plume of smoke he blew at the ceiling. I recognized the smell of Gauloises, a French brand some of the younger professors smoked.

"You tell that to Bump, he will put your typing fingers in a wringer."

"How about this—I quit college because it can ruin

a writer. Smother creativity." I picked up steam as he nodded me on. "Look at Hemingway, Steinbeck, J. D. Salinger. None of them finished college."

"Bravo, Bob Marks!" He rewarded me with a big smile. "If anyone can change Bump's mind about summerboys, it might just be you."

I was pleased by his approval. "You really think so?"

"Indeed, I do. Report to Bump first thing Monday morning. I'll make sure he's expecting you. Don't bother telling him anything. I'll handle it.

"As for the rest of that motley crew, just tell them you've been expelled from college for beating up the dean. Or impregnating his daughter. Something they'll appreciate." He picked up a book and waved me out of the room. "The job is yours if you can hack it."

I was totally confused. "What do you mean, it's . . ."

"Laundry work is no piece of cake."

"I finish what I start," I said. "But what makes you so sure this Bump Ennis is going to hire me?"

"I'll order him to." He toasted me with his thermos. "I'm Roger Sinclair. This dump is mine."

2

I waited to tell my parents about the job until the last minute Sunday night, while they were packing the Square-mobile for the trip back to the city. I was expecting one of their usual Senate Hearings. But after Mom made me promise not to hitchhike with maniacs and Dad warned me about shotgun weddings, they wished me good luck. After all, I had survived a year away at college, hadn't I?

Also, they had other things on their minds. Dad was waiting for a hospital bed to open up so he could have a double-hernia operation, and Mom was getting ready for the final month of the teaching year, her tough-est time. To top it all off, they were both worried about my older sister, Michelle, who was bopping around Europe, stretching her junior-year-abroad program into a year and a half.

It took me a long time to fall asleep. Had I bitten off more than I could chew? I'd cut grass and I'd been a day-camp counselor, and last summer I was a lifeguard at Spiro's Lakeside, but I had never had a real job before. Could I hack it?

I woke up before the alarm and I trotted the entire

two miles along the county road to the Lenape Laundry. I arrived a few minutes before seven o'clock, breathing fast from the exercise and from nervousness.

A short, bald man with a flattened nose and a big, hard belly, a barroom bumper of a belly, was standing on the concrete loading dock checking a list on his clipboard. He glared at me with beady eyes.

"You Marks?" His voice was a growl.

"Yes, sir. Mr. Ennis?"

"Mis-ter Ennis is my daddy—call me Bump. As for you, I'll call you early and I'll call you late, and when Bump says, 'Jump!' you'll ask, 'How high?' You read me, Marks?"

It was right out of a corny war movie. I knew just how to answer. I shouted, "I read you loud and clear, Bump."

Mistake. The beady little eyes nearly disappeared between his fat cheeks and his caveman brows. "A wise guy, huh? Figures. Okeydoke, wise guy, find yourself a corner. I'll take care of you later."

I parked myself against the white wall near the loading dock. I wished I could just melt into the cinder block. Not one of your great beginnings. Bump must be ticked off because Roger Sinclair had forced him to hire me. Look on the bright side. After a start like this, things can only get better.

The Lenape Laundry came to life. Cars streamed into the parking yard and disgorged women of all shapes and sizes and ages, all wearing white uniforms, plain white uniforms without the familiar Indian head on the back. I liked that. The men were special.

As the women passed me to file through the EM-PLOYEES ONLY side entrance, I spotted some good-looking ones my age. A couple of them smiled, and I smiled back. Things were getting better already. Won't be enough nights in the week for the girls I'll be meeting—sweet, uncomplicated country girls who'll appreciate the attentions of a college man, girls who enjoy simple rustic fun, such as rolling in the hay.

I don't know how long I was daydreaming before the wall began to tremble. I heard a deep rumbling, like distant thunder. I peered through a glass windowpane dusted with soap powder. Clouds of steam rose from the machines inside the huge laundry room. I could barely make out the figures in white, loading the washers and driers, pushing carts piled high with laundry, hanging shirts, ironing, stacking, standing at long tables folding and wrapping. No wonder Roger Sinclair had called it a dismal swamp. I tried to imagine how noisy and stinking and sweltering it must be in there.

A black motorcycle roared into the yard and came to a screeching stop in a spray of gravel. A short, wiry guy about twenty, wearing the white Indian-head uniform with black motorcycle boots and a black motorcycle cap tilted over his aviator sunglasses, gave the throttle one last twist, *vroooom!* before he shut down the engine and dismounted like Marlon Brando in *The Wild One*.

As he passed, he looked me up and down through

9

his shades. I felt a chill. Here was a real hardcase. The name embroidered in blue over his left shirt pocket was *Ace*.

I was watching him so intently, I never saw the green-and-white Chevy Bel Air glide in until a guy I knew, Jim Smith, shouted, "Bob! What are you doing here?"

I ran out to his car. "I'm starting today. What about you?"

"Been here four months."

Bump bellowed, "Move it, Smitty."

"Talk to you later," said Jim. He jerked the Chevy away so abruptly he nearly took my arm along.

I went back to the wall. Jim parked and hurried to the dock. He had grown a pot belly since I'd seen him last, during Christmas vacation. Married life. He'd been complaining then that he needed more money than he was getting out of his father's landscape and gardening business. I'd known Jim Smith for about four years. He was the closest thing I had to a friend among the people who lived all year around at Rumson Lake. I was glad to see him at the laundry.

It was about seven-thirty. More men arrived. A tall young guy with a baby face and a body like Hercules ambled up, swinging an old-fashioned lunch pail. He looked friendly. The name on his shirt was *Cliff*.

A chunky redhead passed me with a scowl. *Red*. I figured him for trouble, like Ace. A couple more went up the steps to the dock and I decided to stop making snap judgements. Probably be all wrong anyway. Like I was with Roger Sinclair. Some ivory tower intellectual.

Half a dozen guys in Indian-head whites stood in front of Bump Ennis like an army squad getting its orders from the sergeant. I couldn't hear what Bump was saying, but from the way the drivers grinned and nodded, I got the impression that Bump was tough and funny and fair. A real leader. I was glad I'd soon be on that team.

Suddenly the men broke ranks and stampeded toward the trucks. I thought of war movies where the pilots scramble across the tarmac to leap into their cockpits and get their fighters into the sky before the enemy squadron attacks. Motors coughed and black exhaust fumes smudged the air. Some of the trucks stormed out of the yard and down the highway, others began backing up to the dock to wait their turn to load.

For an hour or so, Bump stomped around the dock barking orders. Loaded trucks pulled out. When they were all gone, Bump glanced at me, shook his head, and sauntered into the building.

The laundry settled down to a steady rumble and throb. Now and then a customer drove in. The sun rose above the huge yellow-and-red metal sign of Lester Smith's Auto Body Repair across the street. The blacktop under my feet began to soften and shift in the heat.

Roger Sinclair's MG snarled into the yard and Boss Tweedy himself stepped out, buttoned down and rep tied, carrying the jacket of a tan summer suit over his shoulder with one crooked finger.

11

He glanced in my direction as he strode toward the main entrance, and I raised my hand to wave. No response. Not even a flicker of acknowledgment. I pretended I was just scratching my head.

I wondered if this was some kind of a test. But what was I supposed to do to pass?

Stand here to show I could take orders and hang tough?

Or march into the laundry after Bump to show him how much I really wanted this job?

Maybe he had just forgotten about me.

Maybe he was hoping I'd get discouraged and leave.

He better not get his hopes too high.

I'm staying here till hell freezes over.

Or lunchtime. Whichever comes first.

"Looks like I'm stuck with you, Marks." Bump was standing in front of me, his clipboard resting against the shelf of his protruding gut. "Go get yourself a uniform from Ol' Swede."

I was through the side entrance into the plant before I realized that I didn't know where I was going. I stopped a woman who was pushing a cart of smelly linen napkins and asked her where I could find Ol' Swede. She pointed her chin toward a wall of steam. "Just follow your ears."

After a few seconds of concentration, I heard a shrill voice rise above the clatter and drone of machines. "If you don't want to work, girls, go home."

I plunged into the wall, toward the voice. I couldn't

see more than five feet in front of me. I imagined it was like flying blind through a cloud bank.

I heard a young woman's voice, quivering with rage. "We want to work, we just don't want to be boiled alive."

On the other side of the wall of steam I saw a tall, gaunt man with a steel-gray crew cut. He was standing on a table, looking down at a group of women. He was shaking his index finger at them. "I tell you one last time, girls, every one of you I could replace in a minute. Plenty of people want to work if you don't."

"Is it too much to ask you to replace that valve before someone gets scalded?" It sounded as though she was having trouble keeping her voice under control. She had blond hair piled on top of her head, blue eyes, and a snub nose. I skipped a breath.

"I'll look at it soon as I can. I got lots of—"

"You've been looking at it for three months. It's time to . . ."

"What do you want?" His skull face was glowering down at me.

". . . put in a new valve."

"I am speaking with this young man, Diana."

"He can wait." Her face was flushed and her eyes glittered and her breasts heaved under her white uniform. My stomach somersaulted.

"I can wait," I croaked.

"I asked you a question, young man."

It took me a few seconds to remember. "Ol' Swede?"

13

He jumped down from the table. "My name is Axel Peterson." His voice rose an octave. "I was born in this country, I fought in the Argonne Forest in World War One, I am as American as you."

"I'm sorry, Bump said . . ."

"You're lucky he's your foreman instead of me, young man."

". . . get a uniform."

Axel Peterson grabbed my sleeve and pulled me into a soapy fog. I heard Diana shout, "Come back here, Axel," and I twisted around to make some gesture showing I was on her side, but she had vanished. Axel dragged me through a maze of grinding and chattering and thumping machines. He pushed me toward a door marked MEN. It opened into a dim, damp, concrete locker room with an open shower stall, two dirty sinks under fly-specked mirrors, a gurgling urinal, and a toilet booth without a door. Breakfast rose to my throat, but I swallowed it down again.

"Women," snorted Axel. "They don't understand the problems."

He unlocked a closet and pulled out a white shirt and white pants. "You'd think that Diana learned something from her papa." He carefully locked the closet before he handed me the shirt and pants. "But she's the worst. A troublemaker." He glared at me. "You better watch out, I got my eye on you, too." He stalked out of the locker room.

The uniform shirt was tight across the chest and

shoulders. The pants were big. I had to roll up the cuffs and hitch the waist into a clump under my belt at the small of my back so the pants wouldn't fall down. I looked like Charlie Chaplin in *Modern Times*, but it would have to do for now. I didn't feel like going after Axel for another uniform. Besides, this one had an Indian head on the back. I was on the team.

I left my civilian clothes in one of the rusty, sagging lockers and went out to the loading dock.

"Shake out the lead, Marks," barked Bump. A boxy, snout-nosed truck was at the dock, rear doors open. Bump was watching baby-faced Hercules take off his shirt as if he were unveiling a statue. "Give Cliff a hand."

We dragged carts of dirty laundry out of the truck. There were no wheels on the bottoms of these carts, and they were heavier than they looked. I had to put on a massive effort just to keep pace with Cliff, who had so many muscles they were jostling each other for space under his skin.

As we dragged each cart over the dock and into the plant, Bump made a notation on his clipboard. Inside, women took over, separating the sheets and pillowcases and tablecloths and napkins into wheeled carts and rolling them into the white inferno. My eyes burned just looking at it.

By the time we had emptied the truck, my shirt was gray with sweat. Some muscles I hadn't heard from in years were registering grievances. Then we reloaded the truck with carts of clean laundry.

When we finished, Cliff wasn't even breathing hard. He looked down at me, and spoke for the first time. "You expect to last around here, summerboy, you're gonna have to do a whole lot better."

He swaggered across the dock, sprang into his truck, and drove off. And I had thought he looked friendly.

I waited until Bump went inside before I plopped down on the edge of the dock and let my legs dangle. It felt good. I thought about the fiery blonde, Diana. I even liked her name. Diana. Proud and classy. Diana, goddess of the hunt. You can hunt me anytime, baby. I'd have to do a whole lot better than that, too.

A whistle blew inside the laundry and women began drifting out the side door, into the yard, and onto the grass. The morning break. Some of them carried soda bottles or thermoses. A lot of them lit cigarettes. All of them had dark half-moons of perspiration under their armpits. Their faces were shiny and their hair was damp and curly.

Trucks lumbered in. I wondered if the drivers had timed their return for the women's break. Jim Smith and Red pulled their trucks alongside the grass and hung out of their doors. In a minute each of them had a cluster of women. You'd think they were giving away Eskimo Pies.

Cliff's truck roared in and screeched to a stop inches from the dock. Cliff jumped out and ran inside. He looked as though he were foaming at the mouth.

I searched for Diana. I was glad she wasn't flirting with Jim or Red.

Bump came out, Cliff ranting at his heels. "When I get my hands on the rat switched hoses on me, there's gonna be blood."

Bump opened the hood and peered into the engine. "You did a good job taping that hose."

The compliment calmed Cliff. "Lucky I knew how. I'd still be out there."

"Cliffie, I was the one switched 'em." Bump drew two nickels out of his pocket and handed them to Cliff. "Here you go, get us each a Coke and I'll tell you what happened."

I spotted Diana, talking to a cute brunette. I tried to get up, but my legs had fallen asleep. By the time I had pinched and pounded them awake, Diana and the brunette had turned the corner and Bump was yelling, "Marks! Got a job for you."

I staggered over. "Yo." I tried to sound eager and cool at the same time.

"Take Number Three across the street to Lester's, have 'im find you some hoses and clamps that'll fit. Let's go, chop, chop."

"Gotcha, Bump." Wobbly legs and all, I sprang up behind the wheel of Cliff's truck, maybe my all-time best move. I wouldn't have been surprised if those were gasps of admiration I heard. The motor was running, so all I had to do was stamp on the clutch, slap the floor shift into first, ease up on the clutch, and roll. I'd have that white wagon humming out of the yard before anyone could ask, Who was that masked man?

The truck stalled.

I tried to start it, but all I got was a metallic howl and a dying whine. I knew I should shut off the ignition and count to a hundred before I flooded the engine, but I didn't have that kind of time, not with the entire female staff of the Lenape Laundry watching me, so I turned the ignition switch and pumped the gas pedal. The engine whimpered and died.

I was surrounded by upturned faces. Some of the women looked as though they felt sorry for me and some of them seemed to be enjoying the show. Diana and the brunette just looked annoyed.

Bump said, "I thought you told Sinclair you could drive a truck."

I almost blurted that I had never told him any such thing. It had never even come up.

"Summerboy," sneered Cliff. "All he can drive is a bargain."

The upturned faces laughed. I hated them all. I wanted to crawl into the back of the truck and disappear into a drift of white laundry.

Bump shouted, "If you can't start that truck you get down from there."

Do or die. I twisted the switch and floored the gas pedal.

Die.

The crowd suddenly parted and a body hurtled through the air. Motorcycle boots clanged on the metal curb step.

"Have no fear. The Ace is here."

All I could see of his face was a reckless grin.

I blubbered, "Can you help me start it?"

"Does Ivory soap float?" He leaned across me and pulled out a little black button under the ignition switch. "Won't start without the choke. Kick 'er now, daddy-o."

The motor roared to life. "Thanks, I—"

"Don't let these hillbillies get you down." He lifted his dark glasses and winked and was gone.

I blotted out the crowd. I concentrated on the simple task of steering the truck out of the yard and across the highway and into Lester Smith's Auto Body Repair.

I stamped on the clutch, slapped the floor shift into first, eased up on the clutch and gave it just enough gas to let it roll across the yard.

Okeydoke.

I pushed down on the clutch as I reached the highway. It was clear of traffic, a straight shot into Lester's yard. I aimed at the huge yellow-and-red metal sign, now glowing in the midmorning sun.

How sweet it is.

I let up the clutch and hammered the gas pedal and blasted off. Everything is going to be all right after all. I'm going to show Bump and have a great summer and get the girl.

I believed that right up until the instant I stepped on the brake pedal and it sank with a sigh to the floor. The truck didn't even slow down until it smashed into Lester's sign.

3

"Are they going to make you pay for the damage?" asked Joanie. She had stopped paddling. The canoe drifted over the moonlit water toward the island in the middle of the lake.

"It wasn't my fault," I said. "The brakes failed. I was lucky I didn't get hurt."

"What did they say to that?"

"I didn't have a chance to tell them. Bump was screaming at me to turn in my uniform and clear the area."

Joanie laughed. "Never darken our doorstep again," she said in a mock-fierce voice.

"Never darken our uniform. Someday I'll tell you what I nearly did in my whites."

I wished I felt as humorous and nonchalant as I hoped I sounded. Joanie probably sensed how upset I really was, but she was a good enough friend to go along with any little game I wanted to play. We had that kind of relationship. We'd been friends since we were three years old, and we'd helped each other through plenty of rough times.

Until we were fourteen years old, Joanie and I sort

of clung to each other because we felt ugly and different. Joanie had a long, crooked nose and I was very fat. Sometimes it seemed like Joanie and me against the world.

Four summers ago, Joanie had a nose job that left her pretty, and I lost more than forty pounds mowing the lawn of a mean perfectionist named Dr. Kahn. Joanie and I went our separate ways after that, trying to make up for lost time. But we were always available for crises.

When Joanie came home for spring vacation to find out that her engagement to a medical student was over, I spent most of the week cheering her up. We bounced around the city, caught some old flicks, and drank gallons of espresso in Greenwich Village coffeehouses.

We had a good time that week, lots of laughs and a few deep bull sessions on sex, love, and the state of the world. I could relax with Joanie. I didn't have to play Captain Cool. I could concentrate on having a good time instead of plotting my big seduction number. We were platonic friends. All talk.

However, there were moments, like this one, the two of us drifting under a warm, starry sky, when it seemed like a waste to be with Joanie.

"What about the guy who hired you?" she asked.

"I feel like I really let him down."

"I'm sure he can get somebody else."

"It's more complicated than that. Let's drop it, okay?"

"Sure. What are you going to do now?" she asked.

22

"Goof off, I guess. Until it's time to fry my brains at Spiro's again."

"I thought you liked that job."

"Lifeguard's the most overrated job in the world. You die from boredom and nervous tension at the same time."

"You had all those girls hanging around."

"They were too young to tango, if you know what I mean."

"I'm sure I have no idea what you mean," said Joanie in that snotty tone girls perfect in college.

"You sound more like Michelle every day."

She took it as a compliment. "You hear from her lately?"

"We got a card from Italy. Now my folks are afraid she'll come home with a *bambino.*"

Joanie snorted. "Parents never trust daughters."

"Sons either. My dad is sure I'll get one of the laundry girls in trouble and have to marry her and quit school. He's got more confidence in me than I deserve."

"He'll be relieved now. Hey, I bet I could get you a job with me at the Lenape Inn Day Camp."

"Those stinky little brats and their—"

"Oh, I forgot, you're this big, tough truck driver, you can't be—"

"We're going to hit the island." It wasn't exactly true, but I wanted to end that train of conversation. I J-stroked until the canoe veered away from the shore.

On weekend nights in July and August, there was usually a lineup of canoes and rowboats. Make-Out Island, we called it. Tonight, a Monday in May, it looked deserted. I wondered if Joanie was also wishing she was with someone else right now.

"Want to ride into the city tomorrow? Mom and I are going to pick up our dresses for the party."

"I almost forgot. Saturday night is La Big Blast. Tell the truth. Do those French exchange students really look like Brigitte Bardot?"

"I'll tell you the truth. They look like they're not interested in gauche American boys."

I splashed her with my paddle and she splashed me back. Somehow we managed to get back to shore without tipping over.

The telephone was ringing as I walked into the house. I'd promised to call my folks after my first day at work, but I'd stalled for obvious reasons. Now I had to face the music. I scooped up the receiver. "Before you get excited, Dad—"

"It is a wise child that knows his own father," said a familiar tweedy voice.

"Mr. Sinclair?"

"I gather your debut today was less than a smashing success."

"I'm really sorry about what happened," I said, "but it wasn't my fault. The brakes just gave way."

"All is forgiven. Come back tomorrow."

"Well, I, uh . . ." I couldn't believe I had heard him right.

"Unless, of course, you're ashamed to show your face. . . ." He let it hang, like a challenge.

"It's not that, but, well, Bump said—"

"I am the boss. Not Bump. And I want a summerboy, a prince in disguise to mingle with the common herd and bring back to me the legends of the laundry. The drivel of the drivers. The song of the sheet."

I wasn't sure if he was mocking me or not. "You, uh, kind of lost me, Mr. Sinclair."

"I want you in there to observe for me. Tell me what's going on. Who's slowing production, sowing discontent. Making trouble."

I still thought he was kidding. "Sounds like a job for Martin Kane, Private Eye."

"I'm serious, Marks." His voice was cold. "These local yokels are thick as thieves, they're all related, and they're all against me because I married the boss's daughter. I'm an outsider. Like you. I need someone I can trust."

"I want the job, Mr. Sinclair, but snooping—"

"Observing." His voice changed again. Now it was warm. It curled out of the phone and wrapped around me. "You've still got a chance to show Bump that summerboys aren't quitters, that they can pick themselves off the floor and come back for more."

"Look, I'm not sure that I'm really—"

"Cut out to do a man's job? Where's the heroic spirit? Did you leave it at the movies?"

I couldn't think straight. My mind was whining like a stalled engine. "Could I call you back after I—"

"No. It's now or never. Do you want to work for me?"

I took the plunge. "Does Ivory soap float?"

4

"Mr. Sinclair said I had to give you another chance," growled Bump Ennis, "but he didn't say I had to do it on one of my rigs. You're Ol' Swede's baby now."

Bump grabbed my shoulders, spun me around, and pushed me into the building. Axel was waiting with a new set of whites. There was no Indian head on the back of the shirt.

"Make it snappy," said Axel, pushing me toward the men's locker room.

The uniform fit perfectly. But the face gazing back at me from the mirror looked ready to cry. To cheer it up, I curled my lip and flared my nostrils and winked. You're Bobo Marks, Private Eye, and this is your toughest case: You've got to make the laundry come clean. The face in the mirror grinned.

So what? Some people will laugh at anything.

"Hurry up, hurry up." Axel grabbed my sleeve and dragged me out into the rising fog of soap. "You're not one of Bump's boys now, you don't waltz around like you please. You got to put in a day's work for a day's pay, you got to punch in and punch out, and if I catch you leaving the floor except during authorized breaks, I dock you. No excuses. If you're bleeding or unconscious call me first. Here. Punch in."

He handed me a tan card. Scrawled across the top was *Marx.* Before I had a chance to tell him he had misspelled my name, he pushed me toward the time clock. I slipped my card into the mouth of the machine. It made a dinging sound as it chomped on the card. I pulled it out. The numbers 7:23 were imprinted in a smeary red ink. Axel snatched the card out of my hand and dropped it into a wall rack filled with other cards. "You're late already," he said. "Let's go. Time is money."

I followed him through the misty maze of clattering and hissing machines to a corner of the main room, where a bunch of old ladies were pressing and folding freshly laundered bed sheets. They worked in teams, and they moved like folk dancers in slow motion, plucking the damp sheet from a canvas cart, spreading it over the padded board of the pressing machine, bringing down the hot lid in a sizzling cloud of steam, moving the sheet into different positions on the board until the hot lid had pressed out all the wrinkles.

Just watching them made me damp and itchy and hot.

Once the sheet was pressed, another ancient team lifted it off the pressing board and folded it. They performed a little folding dance, each holding two corners of the sheet as they backed away from each other with small, mincing steps, then came together to exchange corners, back and forth until the sheet was the size of an unabridged dictionary. They were very graceful and light on their feet.

I thought of Margaret Mead, the famous anthropologist, who was my sister Michelle's heroine. Margaret Mead was always visiting faraway islands and writing about their strange customs and rituals. She ought to come here. The Sheet-Folding Dancers of Lenape. Maybe I'll write it up for *National Geographic.*

The folded sheet was placed on a long table, where another team of old ladies touched it up with a hot iron, stacked it with other sheets, bundled them in brown paper and white string, and piled them into canvas carts according to destination. They were ready to be wheeled out to the dock and loaded on the trucks. Where I should be.

Axel clapped his hands for attention. "Girls?" Nobody responded. Every one of them looked old enough to be Axel's mother, and he looked old enough to be my grandfather.

"GIRLS!" A few heads turned. "This is the young man who caused all that fuss yesterday. We're stuck with him. I need a volunteer to fold with him."

After that great introduction I tried to look lovable, like a puppy in a crowded pet shop window, but the old ladies were all busy rolling their eyes and grumbling and turning their backs on us.

"If I don't get a volunteer, I'm going to pick someone," warned Axel.

I almost walked out right then. It was one thing

to have the foremen hate you, but white-haired great-grandmothers? They were supposed to take care of boys. This was humiliating. I didn't need this. I could be home sleeping or eating peanut-butter-and-cucumber sandwiches or writing short stories about cowboys and Martians.

"Waaaal, somebody's got to do it." One of the smallest and oldest and most hunched up of the folders shuffled forward. Her wispy hair and her creased face were the same shade of white as her shapeless uniform. But her voice was lively. "You just take it easy till you get the hang, sonny. This can be tiring work if you're not used to it."

I swallowed my laughter. She was seventy-five if she was a day. She looked too weak to carry a tune. I nodded politely. "I'll do my best, Mrs.—"

"Lolly. Everybody calls me Lolly."

"I'm Bob Marks, Lolly, and I'm pleased to—"

"Save your breath, sonny."

She waved me into position between a pressing machine and a folding table. We were going to be one of the dancing teams that folded the freshly pressed sheet into an unabridged dictionary. I'll probably fall asleep on the job, I thought. Standing around waiting for Lolly to catch her breath, I'll atrophy from disuse. I'll rust.

She signaled me to lift two corners of a sheet off the pressing board. It was pleasantly warm to the touch, like freshly baked bread. We lifted together and side-stepped away from the pressing machine.

"Just follow me, sonny."

I let myself fall into the rhythms of the folding dance. Forward four steps, touch corners and exchange, back four steps. The sheet got smaller and thicker. We did it again. I can do this in my sleep, I thought. After we finished the first sheet and turned it over to the ironer at the long table, Lolly nodded at me. Okeydoke, I thought. Everything is going to be all right.

The pain began in my trapezius muscles, the ones that connect the shoulders and the neck. Just a little pain at first, no more than a pinch. It'll pass, I thought. Lolly's been doing this since the Fall of the Roman Empire, so how tough can it be? I'm just not used to holding my arms in front of me. Who is? Boxers. Rocky Marciano. Joe Louis. Sugar Ray Robinson. But they only have to keep their arms up for three minutes at a time. With one-minute rest periods. The most they ever fight is fifteen rounds, which is only forty-five minutes of holding up your arms interrupted by fifteen minutes of sitting on a stool drinking water that someone is pouring into your mouth while someone else pulls on your waistband and rubs your back and tells you how terrific you are. . . .

"You're draggin' the sheet, sonny," said Lolly.

I lifted my arms and danced toward her. Two pain crabs gave my trapezius muscles a final bite and began munching down my shoulder blades.

"Higher, sonny, get your arms up higher." Dusty sunlight reflected off her rimless glasses.

The pain crabs scurried toward the small of my back,

where they met. After a brief conference they began tunneling, separately, across the top of my buttocks toward my hipbones.

"Higher."

I forced myself to think of something besides the pain in my arms and shoulders and back.

Orchestra conductors. They keep their arms up, sometimes for an hour at a time. But they swing their arms, they raise them and lower them and wave at the violins and signal the cymbals and finger the flutes. Music makes all the difference. If I had any kind of music, this would be a piece of cake. Rosemary Clooney, "Sailor Boys Have Talk to Me in English," Harry Belafonte, "Down de way where de nights are gay . . ."

"Pay attention, sonny."

Another team of pain crabs chewed up the back of my neck and went for the cerebellum. With a little luck I'd be dead by the morning break.

"HIGHER!"

Burying me would be a problem. They'd need a coffin large enough to accommodate my permanently extended arms. Or they could just plant me in the ground like a tree and hang wet wash on my outstretched limbs.

Axel blew a whistle. Break. I sagged to the floor. The older folders smiled down at me as they shuffled toward the outside door. "You'll get used to it, sonny," said Lolly.

It seemed only seconds before they returned, full

of pep. One of them said, "Oughta shoot him, Lolly. Put him out of his misery."

"He tries, I'll give him that," said Lolly. "But his mind does wander."

I heaved up on rubbery legs.

Wet heat turned my suede desert boots into blotting paper, rotting my toenails. I stood in the puddles of shimmering gelatin that were once my feet, sloshing forward and back, holding the corners of sheets with plastic fingers.

A blond head bobbed by. "That valve is still leaking, Lolly. You better tell Axel that he's . . ."

"Now, Diana, I've been around too long to make a commotion over every little thing."

I noticed a brass valve on one of the pressers dribbling hot water a few feet over Lolly's head.

Diana said, "At least change places with the summerboy. If the valve blows, let him get scalded. You can bet nobody's depending on him at home."

"Waaal, I've gotten this far without being steamed alive," said Lolly. "Figure the good Lord wants me raw."

Axel charged over. "Jibble-jabble, jibble-jabble, let's have less talk and more work, please."

The heat boiled my knees into limp spaghetti, liquefying my bones and cooking my crotch. I felt all my little hairs scorch and fall out. My belly button filled with scalding water.

"You look a little flushed," said Lolly.

"Scarlet," I said bravely, "is my natural color."

Heat oozed up the sides of my body, searing the flesh, driving spikes of fire into my armpits. A stream of molten lava ran down my spine, into my crack, where it barbecued my buttocks. A geyser of sizzling oil shot out of my exploding stomach, up my parched throat, and into my fevered brain pan. My eyes popped out.

After a while, it got worse.

The lunch whistle blew, a silver needle darting through the cotton in my head. I stopped moving, my hands stalled over my head. Lolly took the sheet out of my fingers before rigor mortis set in and steered me across the room and gently nudged me toward the door marked MEN. I walked into the door. Someone opened it for me.

I lurched across the locker room to the open shower stall, turned the cold-water handle, and stuck my head under the nozzle. It didn't help at all, but I was too tired to move.

"Shower ain't worked in years." It was Red.

As soon as he left, I staggered into the toilet booth and vomited. I stripped off my shirt like a used Band-Aid and jammed my face under the faucet in one of the sinks. I turned on the cold water full blast.

Delicious, beautiful, wonderful ice-cold water washed the cotton out of my head and the sand out of my eyes and the mud out of my mouth. A torrent of fresh crystal coursed through my body, dousing the fires. I was alive again!

Axel was waiting on the other side of the locker-room door. "You're slowing Lolly down."

"What?"

"She's not meeting her quota. I might have to dock her."

"She didn't say anything about—"

"She's a good girl, no complainer," said Axel. He stalked away.

Faster. Concentrate. The pain was duller now, deeper in my muscles. I could block it out by focusing all my mental energy on following Lolly, becoming her extension. Arms up. Small steps, back and forth.

I was Lolly's remote-controlled robot. I would have worked right through the afternoon break if Lolly hadn't shut me off.

Ace was in the locker room when I staggered in. "How's it goin', Rockin' Robin?"

The best I could do was, "Awrahng."

"That's what I like to hear. I got a fin on you."

"Whafor?"

"The quitter's pool. Only the Ace bet you would last the week."

"Betting on when I'll quit?" I felt sad and mad at the same time.

"Cliff bet you won't show up tomorrow. Red gave you till Thursday. Yo-yos don't know how tough us city cats can be. If you can make it on the bricks you can make it in the sticks. Right?"

"What did Jim Smith bet?"

"He was against the whole thing." I wondered how he could see me through those dark glasses in the dim light of the locker room. "You feelin' okay?"

"I'm fine."

"Hot in there?"

"You get used to it," I said coolly. "By the way, thanks for trying to help me out yesterday."

"When I saw you plow into that sign, I said, 'Bye-Bye, Bobby.' And I knew they'd try to pin it on the Ace. Then you stepped out of the wreck. Crazy." He shook his head with admiration. "I said to Bump, 'That is one far-out way to convince Sinclair that Number Three needs new brakes.' "

"You mean they knew that truck—"

"Man, everything's wrong with everything around here. But we operate on the golden rule. He who has the gold rules. And Sinclair just don't care."

"Maybe somebody should straighten him out," I said.

"Not the Ace. Bobby-baby, I am just passing through. I got out of Brooklyn two steps ahead of some very large cats packing heat, and as soon as I get the bread I am continuing on to Cal-i-for-ni-a. The laundry's just a pit stop. The Ace will make no waves."

"That's a pretty cynical attitude."

"You be the hero." He cocked his head toward the sound of the whistle ending the break. "Get back in there, daddy." He patted my can like a football coach and shoved me toward the door.

The last part of the afternoon was a blur, a damp, soapy, roaring blur. As long as I didn't stop I felt no pain. Just a crushing numbness in my back and shoulders. I saw everything through a white mist, heard everything through a grinding clatter. The world smelled of bleach. I could have been delirious.

Once or twice, when my mind cleared, I considered turning around and walking out the door. Be doing Lolly a favor. But then I imagined Bump saying to Roger Sinclair, 'That's a summerboy for you,' and I remembered the quitter's pool. Bad enough Ace losing five bucks over me, I hated the idea that Cliff would win a pile.

Lolly pried the corner of a sheet out of my hand. "That was the whistle, sonny. It's all over for today."

"Thangoo."

"Now you go right home, take a hot shower, have a good dinner, and get to bed early. Take some tea with milk and honey, help you sleep. Tomorrow be better. Got to be."

I stumbled into a line of women punching out. Someone helped me slip my card into the time clock. Someone else nudged me out the side door into the yard.

Air!

It felt like an ice pick in my lungs. Then the oxygen hit my brain with the force of a double martini. I began weaving across the blacktop. Cars missed me by inches.

Someone propelled me toward the grassy lawn in front of the main entrance. I walked into a tree. I hugged it and held on, breathing, rubbing my cheek against the rough, reassuring bark. I was still alive.

A woman's voice. "We can't just leave him there, Diana."

"Why not? He's Roger Sinclair's boy. Let Roger Sinclair take care of him."

When I finally let go, the yard was empty. The laundry seemed deserted. I took a deep breath and almost fainted. I took a few shallow breaths, just enough to get me started, and pointed myself toward home. My head still wasn't operating but my legs knew the way.

5

A bird woke me at dawn. Rockin' Robin. I was sprawled facedown on my bed. I was still wearing my white uniform and my desert boots. I hurt in places I hadn't visited in years. But once I was out of bed, moving around, I felt better, and after a shave and a long, hot shower, I was flexing my muscles at the mirror. They didn't look any bigger than usual, but at least the heat of the laundry hadn't shrunk them.

I didn't remember eating dinner when I got home, and when I checked with my stomach it howled and whined. So I had a double orange juice, four scrambled eggs, bacon, three pieces of toast with butter and jelly, two cups of coffee, and a bowl of vanilla fudge ice cream. While I made sandwiches for my lunch, I ate a few slices of salami wrapped around lettuce and Swiss cheese chunks. As usual, Mom had left a full fridge. She always told me to eat a hearty breakfast. Most important meal of the day.

My whites were still soggy and stinky, so I stuffed them into an old paper shopping bag and set out for town. There wasn't much traffic on the county road at six A.M. The dewy breeze caressed my face and hair.

The rays of the sun were just strong enough to take the edge off the early chill and to glaze the rippled surface of Rumson Lake with a silvery shimmer.

I liked the idea of being up and around while most of the town slept. During the school year, I'd seen my share of sunrises, usually after staying up all night to cram for an exam or to have a deeply superficial pseudo-intellectual mental gymnastics match with a college girl who'd read Freud, too. I'd feel cranky and chilled as the sun rose. But waking up early to get to a tough job made me feel lean and clean.

There were only a few women ahead of me as I punched in. I looked up to discover Axel blocking my path. I handed him the shopping bag. "I need another uniform. Please."

He must have been surprised to see me, because it took him a long time to figure out what I wanted. Finally, he said, "One change a week, that's all you . . ." His nose wrinkled as the stench rose from the bag. "Just this once."

Lolly looked as though she hadn't budged since yesterday. She was in her position, under the dribbling valve, holding out two corners of a sheet to me. She was wearing a pink ribbon in her wispy white hair, a pink ribbon tied in a bow. I took the corners and began the dance.

The second day was easier than the first because I knew I wasn't going to die folding. The pain in my arms was less severe because I was expecting it, and the heat wasn't so bad because I knew I had gotten through it once. I was even walking semi-upright when I went into the locker room during the morning break to pee.

Cliff was sitting on a toilet, his white pants around his ankles. When he saw me, he yelled, "Can't you read?"

"What?"

"This is the MEN's locker room." He laughed and squeezed, simultaneously. Very impressive. But cement heads always spoil it. He added: "You belong in the WOMEN's locker room. With all the rest of Ol' Swede's girls."

"Be careful you don't squeeze out all your brains," I said.

He started to stand up. Just in time he remembered where he was and what he was doing.

He flipped me the finger.

"What's that?" I asked as I hurried out. "Your IQ?"

I was back in the fog, congratulating myself for having delivered the perfect squelch, when I realized that I hadn't peed and now I'd have to hold it until lunchtime because Axel didn't allow anyone to leave the floor except during authorized breaks. Big victory.

At lunchtime, I went to the bathroom, then took my paper bag of sandwiches and fruit outside. It was a warm, sunny day. Cliff was pitching a softball to Red. Ace and Jim were holding court from the steps of their trucks, regaling the women with tales of the open road. The women munched their sandwiches and smoked their cigarettes and listened intently, shaking their heads and giggling and murmuring at the heroic adventurers. You'd think it was the Lone Ranger and Buck Rogers between installments. I was glad that Diana wasn't in the audiences.

I finally spotted her on the grass behind the plant, sitting with half a dozen other women. I took a deep breath and casually sauntered over. I didn't have an ice-breaking opening line, but I figured that I could just keep on walking if nothing developed.

The cute brunette raised her head as I approached, and said, "Let's welcome the new contestant to *I've Got a Secret.*"

That threw me. I didn't watch much television, but I knew the program, *I've Got a Secret.* A panel tried to guess some silly little thing about a guest. Like he slept with his beard outside the covers. I wondered if she was referring to something on a recent show. No matter. The ice was broken. My move now.

Be suave. "Nice spot you've got here," I said suavely. When nobody said a word, I plunged on. "You always eat here?"

"Mr. Sinclair ask you to find out?" asked Diana. She didn't sound friendly.

I decided to play dumb. "What do you mean?"

"Don't play dumb," snapped Diana. "We know what's going on. Mr. Sinclair hired you and he wouldn't let Bump fire you after you smashed the truck and he wouldn't let Axel fire you after you slowed the folding line."

"So what?" I was sorry I had started with these harridans. I was getting annoyed.

"So we have nothing to say to spies," said Diana.

Sometimes the best defense is sarcasm. "I'll level with you ladies," I said. "I'm here to write an article for the *Reader's Digest.* It's called, 'How I Saved a Bear Cub, Found God, and Made a Million as an Undercover Folder for the FBI.' "

That would have earned a few chuckles in the dorms, maybe even in English I, but not one of them smiled. They didn't even blink.

"This may all be a big joke to you," said Diana, "but not to us. We work here." The others nodded seriously.

"What do you think I do?"

"Now that's *The $64,000 Question,*" said the brunette. "I think you're a fink for management."

Diana stood up. She was slim, and the top of her blond head only came up to my chin, but something about the pugnacious angle of her body made me want to take a step back. I held my ground and glared right back at her. Her hazel eyes had glints of yellow that matched her hair.

"I don't think you understand what's going on in this place," she said.

"I think you all watch too much television," I said. "What's this supposed to be? *Gangbusters*? *Mr. District Attorney*? or *It Pays to Be Ignorant*?"

Her eyes blazed. Blazed! I winced, imagining my English instructor scrawling CLICHÉ! in blue pencil across my composition if I ever dared write that. But her eyes did blaze, and fiercely enough to make me take a step back.

"We're dependent on this place," she said, "and we're trying to improve our conditions. It's our lives. You're just a summerboy—you'll be gone before it gets cold and you don't really care what happens here. Go back and tell that to Mr. Sinclair."

I didn't know what to do or say. I'd never met a woman like her before, who just stood up like a guy and talked right into my face. The girls I knew might get smart or flirty or even bitchy sometimes, but I never had one go head-to-head with me like this, like we were equals. Except for Joanie, of course, or Michelle, but they didn't count.

If Diana had been a guy I could have told her where to get off or even tagged her one in the chops. Under the circumstances, the best I could do was a weak "You can think what you want."

I turned away before anyone could see my face turn pink. I stomped back into the plant and threw out my lunch.

On the way home that afternoon, I decided to finish the week, then quit. I can work two more days standing on my head. No sweat. Show those hillbillies I can take anything they can dish out and let Ace win his bet. Then Lolly can get a new partner who won't slow her down. Ace and Lolly, the only two people who've shown me squat. My supposed old buddy, Jim Smith, won't even look at me when Bump's around. As for Roger Sinclair,

T.S. I could have been killed on that truck for all he cares. And for all I know it was his idea to put me Inside. Maybe he wants me spying on Diana. If he can't find out for himself what's going on in his own plant, he doesn't deserve to know.

Once I made my decision, I felt much better. My last two days at the Lenape Laundry went by in a flash. I really got into the rhythm of the folding dance. I almost enjoyed it. I started making up little songs: "You fold sixteen sheets, what do you get?" and "Jibble-jabble, Aw-rootie." Just so the week wouldn't be a total waste, I decided to dash off a musical comedy about the laundry, a bigger hit than *My Fair Lady.* I'd call it *Folderol.* I'd send Diana two tickets on the aisle, the best seats in the house, but I wouldn't talk to her after the show when she came backstage to thank me.

I tried to get Lolly to change positions with me. I didn't want her getting hurt while I was there, and I figured I could leap out of the way if that valve ever popped. But she refused. "When you get to my age you get set in your ways, sonny. If I changed places, I'd probably start dropping sheets."

But she was touched. She invited me to eat my lunch with her and her friends.

It was nice. The older folders had their own corner of the back lawn, in the shadow of a heap of rusted, discarded machines. I sat next to Lolly and nodded and smiled while they talked about their knitting and their cooking and their families and their aches and pains. It was like being with my grandmother. I even felt a twinge of nostalgia. One more day and I'd probably never see these people again.

Thursday night my parents called. They were staying in the city this weekend. Did I want to come down? I reminded them about Joanie's party. We talked for a while. I was noncommittal about the laundry. If I told them I was quitting they would have a dozen questions, comments, and suggestions. Mom made me go over what food was left in the refrigerator and the pantry closet, and she dictated a shopping list for the coming week that I could pick up, an armful a day, on my way home from work. I humored her and wrote it down, as if I couldn't figure out my own menus. Dad reminded me not to hesitate calling the Biancos or the Morans or even the Bushkins if I needed any help. I humored him, too. I could take care of myself.

I was extra alert on Friday, my final day, making mental notes. I might write a novel instead of a musical. An author named Evan Hunter once spent about a week as a substitute teacher in a tough high school and then he wrote a best-seller called *The Blackboard Jungle*. I might call my best-seller *The Soapflake Inferno*.

I mentally noted how Roger Sinclair floated through the plant like a ghost, hardly ever talking to anyone except Bump or Axel, his nose wrinkled and stuck in the air as if the smell offended him.

I noted how Axel liked to touch the women as he talked to them, pinching cheeks, patting fannies. Even

46

the older women. But he kept his hands to himself around Diana and the brunette who had called me a fink.

I noted how most of the women pushed back straggling strands of damp hair or hitched up their bras anytime one of the drivers walked into the plant. And how the drivers swaggered around as if they were pilots or movie stars.

All good details for *The Soapflake Inferno,* the kind of details that convince the reader that the author was really on the scene. Even if only for a week.

Just before the four-o'clock whistle, Axel came around with the pay envelopes. I stuffed mine into a back pocket.

"Such a rich fella, don't even count it," said Axel.

I pulled out the envelope and ripped it open and made a big show of counting my money. $27.46. About twenty dollars less than I would have gotten working Outside, on a truck.

"He doesn't trust me, he has to count it," said Axel.

The women were all chattering about their weekend plans as I punched out for the last time. Ace hadn't come in yet from his last run, and Lolly had hurried out to catch a ride, so there was nobody around I wanted to say good-bye to. I just slipped out of the yard and I didn't look back. I might turn into a pillar of soap.

I couldn't understand why I felt so sad as I walked along the shoulder of the county road. Who needs the Lenape Laundry? Half the people there will be glad when I don't show up on Monday morning and the other half won't even miss me. But I did feel low. I'd failed to make the grade at a real job. And I had left behind a few people whose respect I would have liked to earn.

Up ahead, the south tip of Rumson Lake glistened in the late afternoon sun. Mr. Spiro would be painting his rental rowboats for the summer, repairing the rafts and the picnic tables, cleaning up the food stand. I knew he'd be glad to see me. If I could talk him into a cost-of-living raise I might consider going back to work for him. There were worse ways to spend a summer than sitting on a high wooden chair surrounded by admiring females.

Spiro's Lakeside was in sight when a Lenape Laundry truck pulled up alongside me, spraying gravel against my legs.

"Bob!" It was Jim Smith.

"What do you want?"

He jumped out of the truck. "Talk to you."

"You had all week."

"Bump's on my back all the time." There was a trace of a whine in his voice. I was embarrassed for him. "I'm trying to pay off a trailer and a car at the same time. I need the job."

I wasn't about to let him off the hook so easy. "If you're so worried about Bump, how come you're out late with the truck?"

"Gimme a break." He was sweating. "Cathy's almost three months gone. I need another kid like I need a hole in the head." He wiped his right hand on his uniform shirt and held it out. "No hard feelings, okay?"

I shook his hand. "You didn't think I was Sinclair's spy, did you?"

"Don't matter what I think. Bump hates Sinclair, and when Sinclair shoved you down his throat he started to hate you. Nothing personal."

"I'm glad to hear that," I said sarcastically.

"Good." Jim wasn't subtle. "Everybody's real jumpy. The trucks are in bad shape—Bump's been switching around parts just to keep 'em rolling. Sinclair won't pay for no major repairs or any preventive maintenance."

"How come?"

"You hear rumors." Jim shifted the toothpick in his mouth from one corner to the other with his tongue and spat into the dirt. "Ever since Sinclair's father-in-law passed away last year, the laundry's gone downhill. You're lucky to be gettin' out."

"Who said I was getting out?"

"I figured, knowing you." He squinted at me. "Kind of ornery and all. I figured you'd stick the week out to prove your point, but after that . . ." He shrugged.

Everybody thinks they've got my number. Now I really did feel ornery. "I haven't made a decision yet," I said.

"You don't want to stay, believe me." He broke the toothpick between his teeth. "You can get a better job. What do you want to bust your back for? You don't want to do women's work, do you?"

Before I thought it through, I said, "You know what?

I think you're Bump's messenger boy. He sent you out to talk me into quitting, didn't he?"

I could tell I was right. His hands balled into fists and his face twisted into an ugly scowl. But he just turned around and climbed back into the truck. He peeled off in a clatter of gravel and left me with the taste of burned rubber.

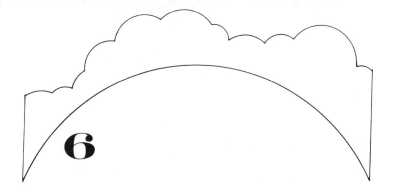

6

I got to Joanie's party early to give her moral support. Also, to get first crack at those French exchange students.

Joanie's father had made a pile of money in the last few years and he wanted everyone to know it. He'd turned his summer place into the fanciest on Rumson Lake. When I arrived he was sitting in a white wrought-iron throne at the crest of his magnificent blue-green lawn, sipping what looked like a double martini. Lord of the Manor. He toasted me with his glass. "Makes it all worthwhile, a layout like this, huh, Bobby?"

"You said it, Mr. Miller." It looked great if you liked southern plantations in upstate New York, which I didn't. The Millers' big white house with its fake columns looked like a miniature *Gone With the Wind* in the fading light. The grass carpet flowed from the house past a new tennis court on down to the renovated boathouse and diving dock.

"Hate to tell you what I spent on the waterfront alone, just laying gravel around the dock so the princess and her mother don't have to"—he raised his voice in a mocking falsetto—"feel all that muck squishing between our toesies."

He toasted his waterfront. In the extra-deep voice he used to deliver Important Pronouncements, he declaimed, "You can have something like this someday. If you're not afraid to be a take-charge guy who grabs for the brass ring."

That was a dig at my father, who refused to quit his job as an accountant with a big company when he had the chance to be partners with Mr. Miller. I didn't want to be disloyal to my father, so I just grunted.

"Better go tell Joanie you're here. She's been complaining I've got more guests coming than she does."

"I thought this was a party for the French girls."

"When you're springing for a bash like this, you want to make it pay off. I invited some people I might do business with. The Mosses—he runs Rumson Plumbing—and that young fellow who married into the laundry . . ."

"Roger Sinclair?"

"You know him?"

"My boss."

Mr. Miller lowered his glass. "At the laundry?"

"I've been there a week. What's the matter?"

He cleared his throat, looked around, and leaned forward so far he nearly tipped off his wrought-iron chair. "You've always been a real smart boy, Bobby. I've told you that plenty of times, haven't I?"

"Actually, smart aleck was the phrase you used."

He guffawed and punched me lightly on the chest. "Listen, this Roger Dodger is up to something. You think he might be cooking his books or skimming the . . . You following me?"

"Not really. I'm an English major, remember?"

"Never apologize." He lowered his voice. "Keep your eyes and ears open for me, willya? Something comes up, even if you don't understand it, make a mental note and let me know. I'll understand it."

I tried not to laugh. "You mean spy on Roger Sinclair?"

"You got it, Sherlock."

I laughed. It was too funny. Spy on the guy I was supposed to be spying for. "You think this is how Nathan Hale got started?"

"Smart aleck," said Mr. Miller, rising. "That was the very phrase. So how about it?"

"Okeydoke." I didn't know what he was talking about, but since I wasn't taking any of it seriously, I didn't think it mattered.

Joanie stuck her head out a window. "BOB!"

Mr. Miller shook my hand. "I better let you go before Joanie comes after my scalp."

I hurried up to the house. Joanie looked terrific. She had a new hairstyle, short and fluffy, and a new dress, a yellow-and-white off-the-shoulder number. She filled it out better than I had ever noticed before.

"What were you and Daddy whispering about?"

"The same old story. Love and glory."

Joanie laughed and gave me back a *Casablanca* line. "Here's looking at you, kid," she said.

53

Her mother marched in. "Joanie? There are guests arriving. Opal needs help with the canapés. Bobby? How's your father?"

"He's still waiting for a—"

"I'll call him tomorrow. Joanie? Are Mignon and Marie dressed yet?"

"I think they're still down at the lake," said Joanie. She made a face at me. "You wouldn't believe their bathing suits. The teeniest bikinis you ever saw."

"Bobby? Be a dear and run down and fetch them."

Joanie said. "You'll never see any of them again."

"Bobby is a sweet, responsible, absolutely trustworthy person," said Mrs. Miller.

"Believe me, I'm trying to change," I said.

Cars were rolling up the driveway, mostly Caddies and Continentals. Mr. Miller was signaling them in with a drink in one hand and a cigar in the other. I hurried down to the dock. Two incredibly gorgeous creatures, gleaming in the last orange rays of the sun, were splayed out on giant white towels. Their bikinis didn't leave much to my imagination.

"Bonjour," I called out.

They both jumped up and waved, as if they'd been waiting for me all their lives. One of them said, "You must be Bop."

The other one said, "I am Mignon, this is Marie."

"Vive la différence," I said. Three years of French were finally going to pay off.

We linked arms on the walk up to the house. I sensed

that Marie was squeezing my arm just *un peu* more tightly than Mignon. Or was that Mignon squeezing? Who cares? They're both so adorable. I got light-headed. I started babbling, "*C'est la vie.* Have you tried the skinny-dipping yet? *C'est magnifique.* Rumson Lake's famous for skinny-dipping. It's in all the guidebooks."

"Skeeny-deep?" They looked puzzled.

"It means, ah, *sans* bikini."

They giggled and squeezed my arms harder. Both of them. Mignon or Marie said, "When?"

When I got my tongue unstuck from the roof of my mouth, I said, "Tonight? When it gets dark?"

Suddenly, they let go of my arms and started running toward the house, covering themselves with their towels as they passed the arriving guests. Marie or Mignon shouted over her shoulder, "See you later, alligator."

I burbled, "After a while, crocodile."

I reached the patio in a daze. "Bobby, I want you to meet . . ." Mr. Miller pushed me toward some man whose name I didn't catch who told me how much he liked my father before he passed me on to his wife, who told me how much she liked my mother, who released me when Mrs. Miller sent me for more club soda. Joanie handed me a vodka tonic and asked me to bring it to Jerry Silver, who was posing against one of the fake columns, practicing his phony charm on some couple who looked as though they had just stepped off a yacht. Jerry had dated Michelle a couple of summers ago when we all worked together at a day camp. I handed him the drink. Before I could escape, he trapped me with his theatrical voice.

"Tell me, Brother Roberto," he said, "is your sister still abroad?"

"She's not abroad anymore," I said. "She's a chick."

The yachting couple looked at each other, unsure if they were supposed to laugh. Jerry smiled. "Sophomoric humor," he explained to them. I could see he had had his teeth capped. I'd heard he had gotten a job in television. "But what can you expect from a sophomore? Where is Michelle?"

"She took a tramp in the woods," I said, moving away.

Mr. Miller ambushed me coming off the porch and sent me to help a woman park her car. She was so grateful she whipped out a fuzzy color snapshot of her granddaughter, a chubby blonde with a beehive hairdo. She told me that the girl had an A average and a cha-cha trophy. Also, she was very sweet and in person looked more like Debbie Reynolds than Debbie Reynolds did. She wouldn't let me go until I pulled out my pencil and notebook and wrote down her number. These things happened to me because mothers and grandmothers and aunts thought I was responsible and absolutely trustworthy, the kind of boy to keep their daughters and granddaughters and nieces harmlessly occupied until Dr. Right showed up.

The fools. If they could only fathom the seething

sewer of my mind. Mignon and Marie and me. The moon will blush and turn aside when we three slip into the soft, lapping waters of Rumson Lake.

An MG convertible came snarling up on the lawn. Roger Sinclair stepped out, very Ivy in a green-and-white cord suit. He checked out the place with the same disdainful expression he wore in the laundry. A short, chunky woman in a gauzy pink dress climbed clumsily out of the passenger seat. She seemed unsteady on her high heels. Her waist was thick, but I couldn't tell if she was fat or pregnant. Her eyes were swollen and red, as if she had allergies or had been crying. I was surprised that Roger Sinclair had such a dumpy wife.

I stepped back into the shadows. I didn't know what to say to him, anyway.

I got down to the lake just as the sky turned navy blue. I left my clothes under the boathouse steps. I was shivering. Goose pimples erupted on my arms. I walked to the end of the dock.

Bop.

Was that a bird, the slap of the water against the shore, or the voice of Marie/Mignon?

I waved toward the sound. I thought I saw two shadows among the trees behind the boathouse. It must be them.

One daring dive would be worth a night of childish seduction maneuvers, hours of touch and go. *Quel homme,* they would sigh, what a man! It would be an insult to trifle with him. Mignon and I would proceed directly to our *grande passion.* Or Marie and I. Or Mignon and Marie and I? *Mon dieu.*

I sprang off the dock.

It was an almost perfect dive. I concentrated on keeping my legs together, and for once I managed to get them both straight up behind me. I plunged toward the water like a rocket.

I knew I looked good. I could imagine Marie and Mignon gasping with admiration. What *savoir faire*, they would agree, what *joie de vivre!*

Just before my outstretched fingers touched the water, I remembered Mr. Miller telling me he had laid gravel around the dock. I had made this dive a thousand times, but always into six feet of water with a muck bottom. It would be shallower now, and the bottom was covered with stones.

I tried to stop in midair. To turn around and go back.

I managed to bring my arms back so that the top of my head hit the water first. I tried to flatten the dive into a bellywhopper, but it was too late. My form was too good. The best I could do was change the angle of impact.

My face slammed into the gravel.

My eyes. I thought about my eyes. The last thing they would ever see was the shadowy shapes of two French girls. And maybe I had even imagined that.

My teeth. Would they all be knocked out? My father

would be furious after he had spent so much money on my braces.

My nose. A mashed pug.

My life. I might never get out of this lake alive.

I expected my past life to flash on the inside of my eyelids. But the last show was my future death.

Two French girls, in black bikinis, bore my body up the lawn. Guests crowded around, drinks in hand. There were murmurs and chuckles.

"He certainly doesn't look like a great lover," said Jerry Silver.

"Cover him, he deserves that," said Joanie, handing Mr. Miller my underpants.

"Fruit of the Loom," announced Mr. Miller, holding them up. "The boy didn't know how to dress."

"And they're stained," said Roger Sinclair. "Would you believe this boy worked in a laundry?"

I broke the surface. The waterfront was deserted. I was alone. I was alive. I could see. I touched my teeth. They all seemed to be in place, and none of them were loose. I could smell.

Then the pain began.

A faint burning, on my forehead, spread to my right eyebrow, to my cheekbone and down to my chin. My entire face was on fire.

I staggered out of the water and into the boathouse bathroom. I turned on the light.

The face that leered out of the mirror was a bloody rag, pockmarked with a thousand bits of stone imbedded in the skin. It was a Halloween mask of a face. A horror-movie face.

"Hi, handsome," I said. The face tried to be brave and laugh, but the best it could do was form a hideous O with its torn lips.

I blinked the grotesque image away. What an imagination that boy has!

When I opened my eyes, the face was still there. My face.

I washed it carefully in warm water. I wiped away the blood and picked off some of the pebbles. There goes my summer, I thought.

I wondered if I would be scarred for life. Would I need plastic surgery?

First thing, I've got to get out of here. I can't let anybody see me like this. What a jerk I am.

I found my shoes and clothes where I had left them, dressed, and skulked through the shadows up the hill. The party was going full blast. Mr. Miller was standing on his wrought-iron throne, making a speech. People were laughing and applauding. Jerry Silver was sitting on a corner of the flagstone patio, strumming his guitar and singing the theme song from the movie *Moulin Rouge.* He was surrounded by women, including Mignon and Marie. They were gazing at him with utter adoration. As I slunk past, I decided they weren't particularly good-looking after all. French girls were vastly overrated.

I sneaked around the house and out to the driveway.

I was standing in a shadow, catching my breath and planning the last leg of my escape, when I noticed a man and a woman talking and laughing in that jittery way people use when they've just met and they're enormously attracted to each other, but a little scared. I'd been there myself a few times.

The woman was slim, and she had short, fluffy hair. It took me a few seconds to recognize Joanie. I tried to make out the man's features, but they were shrouded in darkness. I'll hear about it soon enough, I thought.

They didn't even look up when I tripped over a lawn sprinkler and cursed.

I moved along the county road toward home at a pretty good pace, ducking my head every time the headlights of a passing car came up. I didn't want to scare someone into a tree.

By the time I got home, the blood had bubbled up in all the pits of my face and was dribbling down my neck. I washed my face in warm, soapy water and picked out some more pebbles. My forehead, my chin, and the right side of my face were the worst. I must have turned my head just before impact, saving my nose. Skin was also scraped off my right shoulder, my right hand, my right thigh and my right knee, but I'd done worse than that as a kid, falling off a bicycle.

At first I was glad no one was home. How would I explain such a face? But after a while I began to worry. I wasn't sure what to do. My jaw ached so badly I couldn't chew the sandwich I made. And my face began to get hot. There were dozens of pieces of gravel under the skin, and some of them must be festering.

I poured alcohol onto a clump of cotton and patted my face. It stung. I drank hot tea with milk and honey. Things usually look better in the morning, after a good night's sleep. But I couldn't fall asleep, and as hot spots erupted on my face, an ice-cold panic filled my stomach. I'd heard about infections in the face that traveled to the brain. Bye-bye, Bobby.

At dawn, I put on a clean shirt and went for help.

7

The Bushkins' cottage was a half mile from our house, on an unpaved road at the edge of the woods. When we were small, Michelle and Joanie and I thought of the Bushkins as keepers of the forest.

They were both short and chubby, with friendly round faces topped by curly gray hair. From a distance you couldn't tell them apart. On summer weekends they would sit in the sun on red wooden lawn chairs in front of their little brown cottage, reading books and magazines through identical rimless spectacles. They would peek over the pages as people passed. If it was Michelle or Joanie or me, they would drop their books, jump up, and offer us cream soda and cookies.

Stumbling along the unpaved road in that early, pearly light, I began to have second thoughts about bothering them. I hated to admit my stupidity to anyone. But all the little hot spots on my face urged me on. I could practically feel the microbes begin their inexorable journey to my cerebellum, millions of them, a horde of marauders determined to sack and pillage my head.

I saw no light or movement through the Bushkins'

front windows. They might still be asleep. It wasn't even seven yet, on a Sunday morning. Maybe I was making too big a deal out of this. I walked around to the back of their house. I saw no light or movement through the rear windows, either. Maybe I should go home. There was probably no real danger of infection. The lake was clean—I hadn't peed in it for years. I'd scrubbed my face with soap, dabbed it with disinfectant. What more could a doctor do? I decided to wait in one of the wooden lawn chairs until the Bushkins woke up.

"Who's there? Who is it?" The voice quaked with fear.

"It's me. Bob Marks."

"Who?" It was almost a scream.

"Bobby Marks," I shouted. "I'm sorry. I hurt myself, I—"

A window scraped open. "Come to the kitchen door."

They were both there, small and rumpled, in identical blue robes. They were trembling. I remembered hearing my parents tell stories about how the Bushkins escaped from Nazi Germany only a few steps ahead of the storm troopers and how most of their family and friends were murdered in the concentration camps. Sometimes my father would say that still didn't excuse what Dr. Bushkin was doing now, but my mother would shoot glances at Michelle and me as a signal for him to end that conversation. We knew what he was talking about anyway.

"*Acch*, your face," said Mrs. Bushkin. "Come in."

64

She reached out and pulled me into the kitchen.

"You were shot?" asked Dr. Bushkin, standing on tiptoes to peer at my face. "Is birdshot?"

"Gravel. I dove off the Millers' dock."

He relaxed. "Showing off for the girls?"

"Yes."

" 'S okay. Just so you didn't break your heart." He chuckled until Mrs. Bushkin wagged a finger in front of his face.

They turned their kitchen into an operating room. Dr. Bushkin pushed me down into a chair and aimed a spotlight into my face. Mrs. Bushkin lighted the burner under a pot of water. I wondered if they were going to sterilize scalpels and hypodermic needles. Dr. Bushkin studied my face through a magnifying glass.

"Bobby, I'm afraid you are going to liff." He leaned back as Mrs. Bushkin swabbed my face with alcohol. Without even looking he held out his hand, palm up. She slapped a pair of tweezers into it.

It didn't hurt nearly as much as I'd thought it would. Dr. Bushkin had a great pair of hands, light and quick and sure. I kept my eyes closed most of the time, but even so I could sense his hands descending like birds and I could feel his fingers pinching and spreading and twisting the skin of my face as the steel beak of the tweezers picked out specks of gravel and deposited each with a delicate *ping!* in a little metal candy dish Mrs. Bushkin held out for him. Her other hand mopped bubbles of sweat from the doctor's forehead with a handkerchief.

Sometimes the pebble went *pang!* and Dr. Bushkin would grunt.

Once he took a break. I opened my eyes to see him sipping a cup of tea. So that's why Mrs. Bushkin had boiled water. I felt relieved.

I don't know how long he worked on my face, but when Dr. Bushkin finally leaned back and lighted a cigarette, sunshine was streaming through the window.

"So tell me, Bobby," said Dr. Bushkin, "was she worth it?"

"There were two of them. And I never found out."

He laughed so hard he began choking on cigarette smoke and Mrs. Bushkin had to thump his back. When he regained his voice, he said, "Hokay, Mister Hot Pants. I got most of them out, but not every one. Nothing to worry about. I'll giff you some ointment and some pills."

"Thanks God his eyes and teeth arc all right," said Mrs. Bushkin. "Your parents see you yet?"

"They're in the city."

"You'll have breakfast with us?"

"Giff him Rock Cornish hen, get it, rocks?" Dr. Bushkin cracked himself up. "Or stone crabs. Get it? Stones?"

"What's the joke?" asked Mrs. Bushkin.

"The pebbles in his face? Little stones?"

"Not funny." She bustled away to squeeze fresh orange juice, which stung the inside of my cheek. I must have bitten myself there. She made jelly omelettes and she toasted bagels, which I couldn't chew. While we ate, the Bushkins asked after my parents and Michelle. I told them about my father's hernias and Michelle's expanding European tour.

"Next summer, God villing, we're going back, see who's left," said Mrs. Bushkin.

After a while I said, "I really appreciate what you did for me. I'd like to pay for the—"

"I wouldn't take your money, Bobby," said Dr. Bushkin.

"Let me mow your lawn then. I'll do it during the week, and when you come up Friday night it'll be all ready for you."

"That's not necessary, Bobby, you don't have to—"

"That would be very nice," said Mrs. Bushkin. "Dr. Bushkin shouldn't be pushing that heavy lawnmower around—he's got to take care of his heart. Yes, you do, Dr. Bushkin," she said firmly, wagging her finger. "You've been warned."

Dr. Bushkin sagged, as if some air had been let out of him, but then he puffed up again. "On one condition, Bobby."

"What's that?" I could tell a bad pun was coming on. His face was getting red and he was shaking with laughter.

"You . . . won't . . . take anything . . . for . . . granite." The sentence was punctuated by bursts of laughter. "Get it? For . . . granite? For . . . granted?"

I had to hold him up while Mrs. Bushkin thumped him.

8

Bump saw me first Monday morning. His beady little eyes blinked, like the shutter of a box camera, as I marched into the yard.

I imagined his brain slowly developing the picture his eyes had snapped: the maroon patches of scab on my forehead and cheek and chin; the black and blue and yellow rings around my right eye; the pits, some red, some still black with specks of gravel that Dr. Bushkin said would eventually work their way out. I hadn't shaved, and tiny brown bristles were pushing through the scraped flesh, like weeds fighting their way up through the ruts and rocks of a neglected lawn.

Bump's eyes bugged. He guffawed. "What happened to you?"

"We were playing pinochle," I said, just the way William Holden said it in *Stalag 17*. "It's a rough game."

Bump hooted and slapped his thigh.

Axel spotted me punching in. His eyes lit up his skull face like a jack-o'-lantern. "You been fighting?"

I flashed the V for Victory sign. He shook his head and stalked away, muttering to himself.

Lolly clucked when she saw me. "Oh, I remember the first time Junior came home with a face like that. Nearly forty years ago. Well, boys will be boys."

Axel swooped down. "Jibble-jabble." But he seemed to be almost mimicking himself. "Don't tell me you were fighting in the Dew Drop Inn."

"Okeydoke, I won't tell you," I said.

"I thought so." He flew away.

Women took unnecessary trips past the folding area just to get a look at my face. Even Diana's sidekick made a reconnaissance run. I wondered if Diana had sent her. I couldn't believe it was such a big deal. I guess it broke the monotony.

I went outside for my morning break and stood in the middle of the yard. Jim Smith sauntered over.

"How'd it start?"

Over his shoulder I spotted Bump, peeking at us over his clipboard. "Nothing to it, Jimbo. I just dove headfirst into a rocky situation."

"Damn." He studied my face with admiration, as if it were a work of art. "They're just plain mean at the Dew Drop. How many was there?"

I thought of Mignon and Marie. "Two," I said. When I saw the disappointment in Jim's eyes, I realized it was only right to count Joanie. And the Debbie Reynolds look-alike. "Actually, you could say four."

His face brightened. "What the hoo. Lucky you got out alive."

"I thought so. When I came up for air, I counted my blessings and my teeth." I was being too cute, I knew it, and I couldn't resist.

The whistle blew and I went back inside with the girls. Jim hurried over to report to Bump, who was waiting impatiently on the dock with the boys.

Ace was waiting for me near the folding table. "Hey, daddy, these hillbillies don't want to pay up on the quitter's pool. We might have to use your oriental stuff on them."

"My what?"

"Don't kid the kidder, kid." He made his hands into cleavers and chopped the air. "Only one way you could of whipped all those guys. You register your hands?"

"Yeah, they're Democrats." I tried not to laugh.

"No joke. You could get arrested for carrying a concealed weapon if you don't register them."

Axel swooped. "Jibble-jabble. You get to work. And you"—he cocked his index finger at Ace—"stay away from my gir . . . my workers."

I folded for less than ten minutes before Bump sent for me to help Red load the tractor-trailer. Lolly patted me on the back as if she was sending me off to school. "Be good now. No more fights."

A week before, I had thought loading a truck was backbreaking labor. After a week with the women Inside, it was like a paid holiday. Fresh air, sunshine, and a little light exercise. When we finished, Red wiped his right hand on his pants and offered it to me. "The guys call me Red." He grinned. "Beats me why."

"Bob Marks."

As we shook, he turned my hand over and examined it. "Ace was right, Bump. Knuckles ain't skinned."

I pulled my hand loose. "So what?"

"You didn't punch out nobody." Red grabbed my hand again. His hand was a vise. I gave up trying to get mine back. He studied the fleshy side of my right hand, where it had scraped the gravel bottom. "Sure enough, all scabbed up."

"Ace was right for once," said Bump. "Marks. Show us some of that oriental stuff. Somebody get him a couple of cinder blocks to break."

I had to get out of this fast. "I'm sorry. The true student of the martial arts never shows off."

"When I was in Korea," said Red, "some of the fellas in my platoon took lessons in that stuff. They got different-colored belts. Black was the highest."

"What kind of belt you got?" asked Bump.

Stop it now, I thought, before it gets out of control. Explain it's all a mistake. Make jokes. Tell them you earned the tattletale gray belt for keeping your karate clothes clean. The green belt for paying in cash. The red belt for not fainting at the sight of your own blood.

"It's just not something I can discuss with outsiders," I said.

That struck a nerve. They looked at each other and nodded. Then they slowly looked me up and down. I

71

wasn't sure if they were going to make me a blood brother or stomp me into the concrete like a rotten watermelon.

"Time we put you back on a truck," said Bump. "It's not fitting, you in there with the girls."

The way Bump spat out the word "girls," I felt I had to defend them. "They work their tails off in there," I said.

"Okeydoke, if you like it better Inside . . ." When he grinned, his bald scalp wrinkled.

"I didn't say that."

The lunch whistle sounded, and women spilled out of the plant. Trucks careened into the yard, as if they'd been around the corner waiting for the whistle. Cliff joined us on the dock. He glowered at me. Ace swaggered up and threw his arm over my shoulders. "Introducin' the Dynamic Duo."

"Kiss him, why don'tcha?" snickered Cliff.

Ace said, "Your mother's calling you, Cliffie. Bubble-bath's ready."

"Bump." Diana's voice. My heart stopped. "I'd like to talk with you for a minute."

"I'm real busy now, honey," said Bump.

"I ain't busy," said Red. He smacked his lips.

"It's important." She was standing on the threshold of the overhead door that led out to the dock.

"Later," said Bump, turning his back on her.

I watched Diana take a deep breath, then step out on the platform.

"Hey," shouted Cliff. "Only drivers."

She ignored Cliff. "Bump? There's a valve on—"

"This is off limits to you broads." Cliff took a step toward her. "Back Inside."

I didn't think it through. I didn't think at all. I just reached out and grabbed Cliff's sleeve. "Down, boy."

He whirled on me. "You want it, summerboy? Here and now?"

Red said, "He knows jiujitsu."

"If that's so hot," sneered Cliff, "how come the Japs lost the war?"

"It's time, Bobby-o." Ace pushed me toward Cliff. "Do it, man. Cut that big stoop in half."

Suddenly I was face to face with Cliff. He was at least five inches taller and fifty pounds heavier than I. Plus he had spent his life lifting and loading. What had I done? Flipped pages? Hurled insults? Pushed my luck?

The women surrounded the dock as if it were a stage. One week to the day I had entertained them by smashing up a truck I was going to thrill them by getting myself smashed up.

Run for it, I told myself. Jump off the dock, dash through the crowd, go home. None of these people mean squat to you. You never have to see any of them again. Why should you care what a bunch of local yokels think of you? You could spend the rest of your life in a plaster cast because of a little dumb pride.

"Bump!" Diana marched out onto no-woman's land. "Can't you stop this before someone gets hurt?"

"She's right," I said.

"Scared?" sniggered Cliff.

"Sure he's scared," said Ace. "Scared he'll pound you into a quivering pile of Jell-O."

"Off the platform, Di," said Bump. "Sometimes men just have to settle their problems with their hands."

"Their problem isn't with each other, it's with the conditions in this—"

"Di! Off!"

"Let's go, summerboy," said Cliff.

He towered over me, his arms folded across his barn-door chest. King Kong with a baby face. He was daring me to throw my best shot. If I tried to KO him with a haymaker to the jaw, I'd probably fracture my hand. A kick in the groin would just make him angry. I'd seen his stomach, a waffle grid of muscle.

His only weak spot was his mind. How do you get to that?

In the movie *Bad Day at Black Rock*, Spencer Tracy whipped a town of killers with only one good arm. After that flick played the campus, a few guys in the dorm took jiujitsu lessons. I tried to remember some of the moves they had shown the rest of us. Or at least some of the sayings their teachers had made them memorize.

"I'm waiting, summerboy."

I looked him in the eye. Loudly, I said: "I have never killed a man just for being foolish."

Ace spoiled it. "There's a first time for everything, Bobby-o."

This is some kind of a horrible daydream, I thought.

Hey, Bobby-o. Don't you always win in your daydreams?

"So it is written," I intoned in a deep voice created for Important Pronouncements. "When words no longer bend the heart, then hands must break the bones."

I bent over and rolled my pants to my knee. I pulled off my shoes and my socks. I curled my toes. I peeked up. Cliff was frowning. He looked nervous. Only a lunatic or a black belt would take off his shoes before a fight.

Careful now, Bobby-o. There's a thin line between melodrama and farce.

I raised my arms. "Give me the strength to win without killing."

"Now that's enough," said Diana.

She was standing in front of Cliff. She looked fierce and beautiful. He looked terrified.

"Let 'em fight," yelled Ace. Thanks, pal.

"We're always fighting among ourselves," said Diana. "That's why we never get together to solve our problems."

"What's your problem, baby?" yelled Red. All the drivers and a lot of the women laughed.

A baby-blue Cadillac made a screeching turn off the highway into the yard. The crowd whirled to watch the pretty girl at the wheel bring the big car to a sudden stop.

I noticed one of the office windows open. Roger Sinclair's face poked out. He was staring at the Caddy. I wondered if he had been watching us on the dock.

"Diana is right," I said. I had to repeat it louder to get their attention back. "Diana is right. If the masters of the ancient arts have taught me anything, it is this: All men and women are brothers."

It didn't make sense, but only Diana was looking at me suspiciously.

I reached out for Cliff's hand. He looked panicky. I said, "I won't hurt you, brother," and I shook his hand.

Now the exit, equally crucial in melodrama and farce. I scooped up my shoes and socks and jumped off the dock. I landed on loose gravel that sent splinters of pain up my legs, but I willed myself not even to limp as I strode across the yard toward the Caddy.

I put my hands on the passenger door of the Caddy and vaulted into the front seat. The buttery white leather sighed beneath me. "Okeydoke, baby," I growled, "burn rubber outa here."

"But, Bob, I—"

"STEP ON IT."

I allowed myself one quick glance as we roared out of the yard. The entire staff of the Lenape Laundry was gaping at me in a frozen tableau, mystified, respectful, adoring. What a difference a week makes! I turned in time to see Lester's yellow-and-red metal sign looming up in front of us.

"Oh, no, not again!"

Not again. When you're hot, you're hot. The Caddy executed a shrieking two-wheel turn, landed with a thud on the road, and I was up and away, swinging loose, riding high.

9

"What was going on back there?" asked Joanie.

"I can't do it justice with mere words," said I.

"Some writer you'll make."

"What were you doing there?"

"Well, uh . . ." She stared through the windshield. I'd never seen her at a loss for words before. "I, uh, was in the neighborhood. I, uh, you know, thought it would be interesting to see where you worked."

"The laundry? Interesting? You've passed it a million times. Didn't your mother have her sheets done before you got Opal?"

Joanie stopped for a traffic light but avoided looking at me. Then it sank in. "Your father sent you. He's afraid I'm going to sue him, and he sent you to talk me out of it."

I braced for Joanie's vehement denial, her vicious counterattack, but all I got was a grateful look. "It's true, Bob. How did you know?"

This didn't make much sense. The old Bull Detector was ringing in my brain, but the Karate Kid was flying too high to pay attention. Who cares why she showed up in the nick of time. Be glad she did. An English instructor would scrawl DEUS EX MACHINA! for an unexplained, illogical rescue. Worse than a CLICHÉ! Let the instructor fight Cliff.

"Hey, tell your old man not to worry. We kill or we forgive, but we never sue."

"I knew you'd say that."

"Say what?" Was she listening to me?

"Does your face hurt, Bob?"

"I actually forgot about it for a while." My scabs began to itch, reminding me that I resembled Franken-stein.

"You sounded so awful on the phone yesterday," said Joanie. "I was really upset when you said you went to a doctor. Until you told me who it was."

"Dr. Bushkin's a doctor."

"A criminal more like it." She changed the subject. "Were you drunk?"

"I forgot about the new gravel."

"Daddy said he specifically warned you that . . ."

I changed the subject. "Tell me about the rest of the party."

"Bob." She looked at me so long and dreamily she nearly drove off the road. "It . . . was . . . wonderful."

"Here we go again, kid," I rasped, to hide the jealous stab I always felt when Joanie fell in love.

She pulled off the road. We were right outside town, along a stretch of meadow. There was nobody around except for a few cows, and they were out of earshot. But Joanie lowered her voice.

"It's stupid, Bob, you're going to tell me it's crazy, destructive, I know it, hopeless, a mistake from the start."

"Sounds serious," I said. "Who's the guy?"

"I can't tell you," she said.

"You've got to be kidding. You've told me in minute detail about every guy who ever looked at you."

She turned to the cows. "Bob, something happened, something I can't even talk about, but I had to tell somebody that something happened that I can't even talk about. Do you understand?"

"I understand that I don't understand."

"I knew you would."

I checked her face for even the trace of a smile. She was very serious. "So," I said, "we both took hard falls Saturday night, me literally, you figuratively."

"Are you making fun of me?"

"You heard the muted moans of the saxophones, the moon hit your eye like a big pizza pie, zing went the strings of your heart."

"Get out," she snapped.

"In the middle of nowhere?"

"You can walk home from here."

"I've got to get back to work. My lunch hour's almost over."

"Oh. The laundry." She started the car and made a screaming U-turn back onto the road, toward town. "I'm sorry, Bob, I really am. It was a mistake to confide in you." She gritted her teeth for the rest of the ride.

When we got to the laundry, I said, "You can drop

me out front," but she drove into the yard and rubber-necked, as if she was trying to look through the windows.

The women were back Inside, but Bump and the boys were on the dock. They elbowed each other and grinned and pointed as Joanie pulled up.

I vaulted over the passenger door, landing heavily on loose gravel again. What is it with stones and me?

"Next time, I hope you drown." She spun the Caddy so sharply she nearly hit me.

I managed to scoop up my shoes and one sock as she pulled away. Good enough. I put her out of my mind as I strode to the dock. Ace flashed me the V for Victory and Red gave me the thumbs up and even Jim was nodding approval.

"Turn in that uniform," growled Bump. "Tell Ol' Swede you're one of Bump's boys now."

10

I was one of Bump's boys. I wore Indian-head whites and hung out of delivery trucks, a toothpick in my mouth, a red Lenape baseball cap pulled low over my eyes, waving to girls along the route. Most of them waved back. It was nearly as terrific as I'd thought it was going to be. I was only a swing helper, loading trucks and going out when a driver needed a hand, but I was on the team. I was Outside.

I'd swagger into the yard about seven-thirty, long after the women were Inside. The plant would be trembling and the windows soap fogged. I didn't bother to punch in. Bump's boys didn't have to hit the clock so long as they toed the line for Bump.

If we had loaded the trucks the afternoon before, we'd stand on the dock, smoking and shooting the bull while Bump and Axel rechecked the loads against the lists on their clipboards. I liked those times in the morning, before the sun got hot, in the company of other men in the same uniform, buddies staying loose until it was time to roll out.

Most of the time they talked about how much they had drunk the night before, and how they had driven home blind and woken up with a tongue that felt like twenty miles of dusty road. "I got so plastered last night," Red might say, "when I got home I kissed the cat and put my wife out on the porch," and everybody would nod and chuckle as if they had never heard that before.

They talked baseball. Jim was a Yankee fan and Ace loved to needle him about last year's World Series, which the Brooklyn Dodgers won. After a couple of minutes of this, Red, who was a New York Giants fan, would say that Willie Mays was a better center fielder than either Duke Snider or Mickey Mantle. They would argue until Bump rapped his clipboard against a wall and said: "Joe D. was the one, boys. After the Clipper, they broke the mold." There would be a hush, as if Bump had invoked a saint.

The first few times I heard all this, I was fascinated, especially since they were playing to me, a new audience. But after a couple of weeks, it got boring. It was just morning calisthenics for their tongues.

Cliff avoided me the first few days I was Outside, but then one morning he gave me a curt nod to show he was willing to let bygones be bygones, and I returned the nod to show I didn't hold a grudge. Nobody ever mentioned our near fight.

Of all the drivers, Cliff was the only one I actively disliked. Red and Ace egged him on, but it was Cliff who usually started the raunchy comments about the women Inside. He would glance in and catch sight of one of the younger women bent over to unload a washer,

her white skirt spread tight across her rear end, and say, "How'd you like to boff that black and blue?"

"Listen to Don Juan," Ace might sneer. "Next time you get any, Cliffie, be your first."

"There's one for you." Red cocked his index finger and fired an imaginary bullet into the plant. We all followed it in.

Diana was pushing a canvas cart toward the washers. She walked erect, her breasts straining against the front of her uniform. I got warm just looking at her through the mist. She tossed wisps of blond hair out of her eyes with a little motion of her head that caused several vital organs in my abdomen to collide. We hadn't said a word to each other since the encounter on the dock with Cliff, but I'd found out her last name by checking her time card. Cooke. Diana Cooke.

"I gave her a chance," said Ace, "but she hates men."

"Maybe she just hates you," I said.

Cliff laughed, a honking sound. "Hear your buddy, Ace?"

"She's a troublemaker," said Red. "Always trying to get the girls stirred up. Ol' Swede would can Diana in a minute if he could. But Bump won't let him."

"Why not?" I asked, hungry to learn more about Diana.

Jim came up the steps. "What's the skinny on Number Six?"

"Lester's looking at it," said Red. "Suspension on

that baby's so bad, you drive over a dime you can tell if it's heads or tails."

I wanted to get the conversation back to Topic A. "What's Bump got to do with her?"

"Who?" asked Jim.

"Diana Cooke." Just saying her name tickled my scalp.

"Don't know her place," muttered Jim.

"Bump and her daddy were army buddies," said Red. "After Cookie wracked up and Sinclair let him go, it was Bump who got Diana the job here. Bump was Diana's godfather."

Before I had the chance to pursue that, Ace said, "If Bump stood up to Sinclair like a man, these trucks would get fixed."

"Believe me, he tries," said Red. "Sinclair just don't care."

Then Bump roared, "Okeydoke, you clowns, mount up and move out," and we scrambled for the trucks.

It wasn't really much of a scramble while I was doing it, just a jump off the dock, a few running steps across the asphalt yard, and up into the helper's side of a truck, but remembering how it looked that first day, I felt like Lt. Rob Marks racing across the tarmac with his squadron to get his pursuit plane into the sky before the enemy hit.

From the Inside it had seemed so romantic and exciting to be Outside. Now that I was Outside, I realized it wasn't all that great. But knowing that the women Inside thought being Outside was great made it better than it really was.

The first morning I went out as a helper, riding with Red, I was surprised when he drove right into town and parked at the Rumson Diner. Two other Lenape trucks were already there, along with a tow truck from Lester's and a flock of pickups and panels. Ace was sitting at the counter with some guys from the lumberyard and the gas company. He swiveled on his leatherette-topped metal stool and waved us over as if we hadn't just all been together on the dock.

Red and I sat down at the counter. When a waitress came over, Red leered up at her and said, "What you got for me today?"

"Read the menu, honey. Or does it sprain your lips?"

Red chuckled. "Say hello to Bob Marks. Just started."

"Hello, Bob Marks." She studied my face. "Who you been kissin', cousin? Grizzly bears?" She gave me a sexy wink that made my scabs burn. "You better dump these bozos before you end up bad."

Ace shouted, "End up in bed, you say?" and the guys pounded the counter until their coffee mugs danced. The waitress winked again and flounced off to the kitchen.

"She likes you," said Red.

"Can't blame her," I said casually.

We usually spent a half hour in the diner, eating doughnuts and swigging coffee, gossiping, telling jokes, kidding around with the waitresses, arguing over which songs to play on the jukebox. Ace would try to play Elvis Presley, but Jim and Red and Cliff would start hollering for Hank Williams, and they'd usually win. Ace was good-natured about it, especially since the other drivers were paying off on the quitter's pool. I think he might have suggested that if they tried to welsh he'd have the Karate Kid collect.

While some of the other guys had second breakfasts, the most I had was a doughnut dipped in lukewarm coffee. The inside of my mouth was still too tender for anything hot or acidy, like orange juice, and my jaw was too sore to chew properly. At home, for breakfast, I'd throw three raw eggs, eight ounces of milk, four heaping tablespoons of chocolate ice cream, a banana, and wheat germ into the blender and whip up Chef Bop LeMarques' Breakfast Soup. *C'est si bon!* Once I put some peanut butter in, too, but it clogged the blender blades. Too bad. I missed peanut butter more than I missed steak. The only time I ever envied Cliff was when he slathered peanut butter on his toasted corn muffin at the diner.

Sometimes, loafing in the Rumson Diner, I thought about Lolly and the women Inside, the heat and the leaky steam valve and Axel on their necks, and I felt a twinge of guilt. But I didn't invent the system. They were folding sheets before I was born.

Since I was the swing helper, I got to go on all the different routes. Ace had the hotels and restaurants around Lenape Falls. Cliff delivered to the mental asylum at Grantsville and a private hospital for rich alcoholics and a conference center for corporation executives. Red had the residential run. It was wasted on him. Housewives came to the door in their negligees. Red just gawked at them, no finesse at all. Not that I did much better, breaking out in a cold sweat when they made eye contact with me.

Jim thought his route, the mansions around Lenape State Park, was the worst. The servants treated him like a mustard stain and never even offered him a glass of water. But I liked that run. Those butlers and housekeepers with their British accents and their snooty ways gave me a laugh. And some good material for my notebook. One advantage of being a summerboy was knowing I didn't have to take their bad manners personally. In a few months I'd be back in college while the butlers and the drivers remained behind.

The first time I rode with Jim I made him stop at the State Park Lookout. Lenape County was spread out before us, the Falls to the east, diamond-tipped water dashing over gray rocks, Rumson Lake to the north, a glittering blue splotch among neat squares of green-and-brown farmland. From the south, clusters of summer homes were advancing on the checkerboard fields. Every year there were more summer homes and fewer farms.

"C'mon," said Jim. "Bump's got the clock on me."

"What's he got against you?"

"Goes way back. Bad blood between him and my

old man." Jim shrugged. "You got to live in a small town to know how mixed up everything gets."

We got back into the truck and Jim eased down the mountain road. He always drove slowly and quietly in the park. It was too beautiful a place to grind gears or burn rubber.

"Why'd Bump hire you in the first place?"

"Sometimes I think he did it just so's he could get back at my old man by busting my chops."

June flowed along and so did I. Up early, shower, carefully shave around my last couple of scabs. Once I started eating solids again, I'd put away a monster breakfast, drop a log, and trot the two miles into town. My calf and thigh muscles were turning to rock. If I ever learned karate I'd be able to kick down brick walls. Bump didn't trust me behind the wheel of a truck yet, but I figured that was only a matter of time. That and my name embroidered on my shirt.

I tried a few times to start conversations with Diana, but she cut me dead. I'd ask Lolly to put in a good word for me, but Lolly would shake her head and say, "She's not your type, sonny," and ask me about the mansions. The other older folders would crowd around and I'd regale them with tales of the open road, creating little dramas that might have happened over the tablecloths or bedsheets. They'd be enthralled until Axel swooped down, crying, "Jibble-jabble, jibble-jabble," and chase them back to work.

From time to time Sinclair nodded at me or raised his eyebrows or gave me ironic little salutes, but we never talked and he never summoned me to his office to hear my observations. I had the impression he was avoiding me. Once, when we nearly collided outside the locker room, I said, "I think we should have a talk."

He recoiled. "Why?"

"I've found out some things."

He stiffened. He glanced around to make sure we were alone. "Well, ah—"

"People are very upset. There are dangerous conditions. There's a valve on the presser that—"

"Oh, that." He relaxed. He gave me his crinkly-eyed smile. "Marks, old chap, you've got to learn that the hero walks through the crowd without becoming one of the crowd."

"What?"

"Don't they teach Thomas Carlyle in that college of yours?" He was laughing at me. "The hero is a messenger from the great unknown with tidings for the common herd. Sort of a super summerboy."

"It's no joke, someone could get badly hurt."

"This is no slave camp, Marks. The characters in this proletarian novel you're writing are all free to leave. As are you."

He turned and walked back to his office. What was eating him? Or didn't he care about anyone but himself?

On the way home from work I usually stopped off at Spiro's Lakeside for a dip and some conversation with

Mr. Spiro. He offered to keep the lifeguard job open to the last minute, to just before the July Fourth weekend, but I told him I planned to stay at the laundry. If I had any doubts, they were erased after I checked out the Lakeside's fresh crop of summergirls. Even younger than last year. You could go to jail for dreaming about them. They were what Red called San Quentin quail.

After swimming, I'd pick up some groceries at the store across the road and trudge up the hill for a wholesome homemade dinner, hamburger or minute steak with a huge salad, lettuce and cucumbers and green peppers and radishes and tomatoes and scallions. All washed down with iced tea or lemonade. Half a cantaloupe or some watermelon. Grapes. Ice cream. My favorite cookies, chocolate chip or Vienna fingers. After a few weeks, I noticed my uniform was shrinking around the waist. I made a mental note to cut back on the salads.

After dinner I might take a stroll, cut the Bushkins' lawn, cut ours, or just stand in back of the house and look down at the winking campfires around the Lake. I'd feel lonely then, aching for a girl to hold, or at least talk to. Now and then I'd walk back down to the Lake to see who was around, but compared to Diana, every girl seemed silly and shallow.

Without wheels, I'd never see Diana after work. What I wouldn't have given for the Squaremobile. I'd find out where Diana lived and haunt the neighborhood. I'd circle her house every night, I'd pop in at the Bowl-O-Fun and the miniature golf course and the Sweet Shop, until that magic moment when I'd spot her, leap out of the car, and suavely say, "What an amazing coincidence, meeting you here!"

Once I looked up Cooke in the telephone book, but there were six of them and I didn't know her father's first name. I had no idea what I would say if I found her number and I called and she answered. I felt hot and cold and damp and dry just looking at the name Cooke. What if she answered, heard my voice, and hung up? What if her father answered and said she was out and I had to spend the rest of the night imagining her in the backseat of some local greaser's car?

Mom and Dad came up a few times in June, brief visits to inspect me and the house and to restock the fridge. They were so preoccupied with school and work and Michelle and the operation that I was able to pass off the last few marks on my face as scratches I got berry picking. They wanted to believe me.

I called Joanie a few times, but she was always out. The last time I called, her mother said, "I thought she was with you. The party at Spiro's."

I recovered fast. "Right. She'll be after my scalp. I better get down there, glad you reminded me."

"You forgot?" Mrs. Miller didn't sound convinced.

"I'm a little confused. I just heard from the folks. Dad's definitely going in Thursday." At least that was true.

"I'm sure you're all glad that's finally settled. It's a shame he'll miss the July Fourth holiday."

"Well, he just wants to get it over with now. I was thinking about how I'd get in to see him, and I forgot all about meeting Joanie. Better go now. 'Bye."

I couldn't be sure if she believed me or not. But that was Joanie's fault, using me as a cover without clueing me in first. Her big romance was more than a month old now. Must be hotter than ever. I wondered who the lucky guy was.

I ran into Dr. and Mrs. Bushkin out walking a few times and they always complimented me on how nice their lawn looked. Dr. Bushkin would shine his flashlight into my face to examine the fading marks and Mrs. Bushkin would invite me back to their house for cake and milk, sometimes for dinner. I always came up with an excuse. I was getting to enjoy being all by myself.

I'd never lived alone before. I liked talking to myself and walking around the house naked and blasting music and not having to think about anything but myself. I'd brought up some records, mostly Mozart and Beethoven, and some books, Faulkner and Henry James and Dostoevsky, to prepare for the sophomore load of music and literature courses. But by the time I settled down at night, I was in no highbrow mood. I usually fell asleep reading a hard-boiled detective novel while some lovesick fool moaned on the radio.

11

I was driving a hearse packed with gravy-stained sheets through a tunnel. There was a light at the end of the tunnel, a neon light blinking the words COOKE'S BODY SHOP. I stamped on the accelerator because I was running late. Bump had the clock on me. The accelerator went right through the floorboard and I suddenly realized the light was the sun and the tunnel came out on the side of a cliff, with nothing below but a thousand-foot drop to jagged rocks, and I jammed on the brakes but they sank with a sigh and the hearse flew out of the tunnel toward the sun. I thought I might make it, keep flying until I reached the opposite cliff, but then the hearse tipped forward and began to fall end over end, black bags of laundry dropping out the rear door, a pillowcase billowing out like a parachute, I couldn't reach it, I tried, but I was falling toward the jagged rocks and I . . .

"BOB!"

I sat up, slick with sweat, my heart rattling against my ribs. I was half blind with sleepers and the dazzle of a bright morning sun. I blinked until Joanie's face swam into focus. It was pressed against the screen of my bedroom window.

"It's me. You having a dream?"

"Yeah. I was going off a cliff."

"Falling dreams are all sexual."

"Same to you, Dr. Fraud." I scrunched under the top sheet.

"Get up! I've got to use your phone."

"You mean Daddy hasn't put a phonsie in your car yet?"

"Bob, the grass is all dewy out here and I'm in a hurry." Her voice was high and querulous. "Can I use your phone or not?"

"It's may I, not can I," I grumbled. "Go meet me at the kitchen door." When she stayed at the window, I added, "I'm not getting up till you go."

"Don't you have anything on?"

"I've got the radio on. Now go."

"You sleep in the nude? That's why you have all those horny dreams."

"Will you just go!" I waited until she left before I got out of bed, stiff as a stick.

I splashed some water on my face and stepped into swim trunks. Joanie was at the kitchen door, impatiently tapping a fancy little straw shoe. She was wearing yellow shorts and a skimpy halter. Lots of flesh showing. She peered at me through dark glasses. Very French Riviera. Her hair was carefully fluffed out. She was wearing a ton of makeup for a Saturday morning around Rumson Lake.

I opened the door. "Where you going all dolled up?"

"To the telephone." She swept past me. I caught the scent of a perfume called Tabu. My sister wore it on heavy dates.

I followed Joanie into the living room. She started to dial, then glanced over her shoulder at me. "A little privacy, please?"

"Make yourself at home." I edged away, but not out of earshot.

I heard her whisper, "Fifteen minutes, darling," and hang up.

"Want some coffee or something?" I asked her.

"No time. If you get dressed fast, I'll drop you off at the bus depot. It's on my way."

"I'm not going into the city today."

She frowned. "How come? Aren't you going to visit your father?"

"Mom called last night, he's still groggy. I'm going tomorrow. Why? Am I supposed to be covering for you?"

"Why are you so hostile, Bob? I thought we were friends."

"Don't you think it's time you told me what's up?"

"Only if you promise to help." When I nodded, Joanie began dialing another number. "When my mother answers, ask her if I've left yet. Tell her you're all ready to go to Lenape State Park for a picnic with some college friends."

"But I—"

"Here." She thrust the receiver into my hand. Automatically, I put it to my ear. Almost immediately, a slightly throatier version of Joanie's voice said, "Hello?"

"It's Bob, Mrs. Miller. Joanie still there?"

"Why, no, Bob, she's already left. She should be there by now." I could hear her voice shifting into the sly gear. "I do hope the weather holds for you. You're going up to the Falls, aren't you?"

Tricky, tricky, I thought, but I kept my voice neutral and dumb. "No, we're going to Lenape State Park. Meet some guys from school."

"Oh, of course, Joanie told me. Well, have a good time and drive carefully. Would you have Joanie call me when she gets to your house? Otherwise I'll worry all day. Bye-bye." She hung up before I could say good-bye.

"Well done," said Joanie. "I'll bet she wants me to call her when I get here."

"Now I know where you inherited all your wiles."

"At least I got something from that woman." Joanie sat down heavily on the sofa. She took off her dark glasses to wipe her eyes, and I noticed the dark circles. Under her tan and her makeup, she looked pale and tired.

"She suspects something, doesn't she?"

"She does. But she's never asked me a direct question. She's afraid I might tell her the truth and then she'll have to deal with it. Oh, and she's simply not up to that, oh, no, not when there's so much redecorating to do."

"Sounds to me like you want her to find out the truth."

"Sounds to me," she mimicked, "that you're Dr. Fraud now."

"Okeydoke. No more cheap psychoanalysis," I said. "But weren't you taking a big chance? What if I'd gone into the city already? What if your mother called the hospital to talk to my folks and I was already there?"

Joanie shrugged. "I did the best I could. I made sure she called your father last night, and I came here as soon as I could get away. But sometimes in life you've got to take chances." She looked me in the eye. "If it's important enough."

"Who's the guy?"

"I'd tell you if I could."

"What's the big deal? Is he an all-year-rounder? A beatnik? Is he Negro?"

"Believe me," she said softly, "that would be easier."

"Easier than what? Hey, Joanie, what did you get yourself into?"

She shook her head. "It's wonderful and it's terrible. He needs me so much. His life is such a mess. He calls me his single candle."

"Sounds like you're playing with fire," I said. "Okay, what do you want me to do?"

She smiled. "I always knew I could count on you. First of all, be careful answering the phone today. It might be my parents checking up. If you're not sure, disguise your voice. Like we did when we were kids."

"You don't expect me to hide in the house all day?"

"No, but keep your eyes open. They've got friends coming up from the city, so they'll probably be home all day. But you never can tell about my father, he might suddenly decide to give them the Rumson Lake grand tour."

"I hope you know what you're doing."

"Oh, Bob, it's beautiful and it's impossible." Her voice quivered. I'd known her long enough to know this was no act. "We've been meeting in the shadows, but today we're going to be in the sunlight, the entire glorious day."

"You better call your mother back."

I walked into the kitchen to make breakfast. Her voice on the phone was high and falsely cheerful, and although I didn't catch all the words, I heard her tell her mother something about stopping along the way at the fruit and vegetable stand for the most scrumptious tomatoes you've ever seen for the picnic at Lenape State Park. She said that at this very moment Bob was eating one like an apple. Good detail, I thought. Just what a writer needs.

12

I went back to sleep after Joanie left. In the afternoon I walked into town. Diana might show up at the annual July Fourth carnival. Besides, I had nothing better to do.

I got to Memorial Field in time to watch them unload the donkeys for the game between the Rumson Lake Volunteer Fire Department and the American Legion post. Some local guys were heckling a farmer who was trying to coax a chunky brown donkey out of a horse van.

Other summers I would have felt shy about joining them, but with my Lenape Laundry baseball cap pulled low over my eyes and a toothpick in my mouth, I almost felt like one of the pack. Red gave me a little salute as I sauntered up, and one of the lumberyard guys I knew from the diner nudged me and said, "This is better'n the game."

The donkey planted his hoofs on the ramp, showed his teeth, brayed, and farted. The farmer's face turned red with frustration. He looked up at us and shouted, "This must be a really big show for you punks."

In the moment of silence, I shouted back, "Yeah. We didn't know it took a jackass to move a donkey."

The guys heehawed and slapped my back. At first I felt good, and then I felt ashamed. The farmer was only trying to do his job.

We drifted over to the refreshment stand and bought beer and hot dogs. We watched the crowd fill the rickety wooden stands and set up folding chairs along the foul lines. Jim Smith ambled up with his wife, Cathy. She looked very heavy for being only four months pregnant. She had a dribbly little kid wrapped around her leg.

"This here's Terry," said Jim, peeling off the kid, who started to whine. "Say hello to Bob."

The kid dribbled at me and I patted its head. I couldn't tell if it was a boy or a girl. "Looks like a real sharp kid," I said lamely.

"Terry talks a blue streak," said Cathy. "At home."

We made awkward conversation about people we knew in common. I told them about my dad, and Jim told me about his cousin, Willie Rumson, who was doing all right for a change, working on his brother's farm upstate.

"Hey," said Jim. "There's your girl friend." He pointed across the field. Diana was pushing a man in a wheelchair.

"You got to feel sorry for her," said Cathy. "But she always did have her nose in the air. Thought she was hot stuff."

"You know her real well?" I tried to sound nonchalant.

"In high school," said Cathy. "Thought she was go-

101

ing to be Florence Nightingale or something. She was all set to go to some special nursing college in the city when her father got hurt."

"What happened?"

"Way I heard it," said Jim, "he cut the rig hard to miss some kid on a bike, and blew a tire. Flipped over. Took the Volunteers three hours to chop him out. Lucky he's alive."

"Paralyzed from the waist down," said Cathy. "Diana has to do everything for him."

"Think I'll go over and say hello," I said.

"You're wasting your time," said Jim.

"Believe me, she's not your type," said Cathy.

Diana and her father were behind home plate, protected from foul tips by the chicken-wire backstop screen. She was even prettier than I remembered from the plant. I'd never seen her with lipstick and eye shadow, or with her blond hair loose to her shoulders. She wore a pink blouse and white toreador pants and pink slip-on shoes. She had a gold chain around her ankle. Her cute little behind hung over the edge of a bleacher plank. I got hot looking at it.

I sat down next to her. "Hi."

She didn't look at me. "Hi."

The crowd roared as one of the donkeys paused on the pitcher's mound to relieve himself.

That great wit, Bob Hope Marks, quipped, "Makes you thankful donkeys can't fly."

Diana didn't react, but her father whooped with

laughter and twisted around. His eyes widened at my cap. "You drive for Lenape?"

"Helper." I reached across Diana for his outstretched hand. "Bob Marks."

"Call me Cookie. How's old Bump treating you?"

"More like a treatment than a treat."

Cookie laughed himself into a coughing fit. "That's old Bump for you. But let me tell you, he'd give you the shirt off his back if he thought you needed it."

Diana snapped, "Just don't expect him to stand up for you."

He leaned across Diana to get closer to me. "She's Inside, never tells me what's going on Outside. Hey, switch seats with Di so I don't have to lean so much."

Diana shot me a dirty look, but she stood up so I could slide behind her to the end of the plank next to Cookie's chair. "Tell my father how you crashed the first day on the job."

"Could happen to anyone," said Cookie.

"My brakes faded out," I said.

"You're lucky," she said, glancing pointedly at her father's wheelchair. "When he had his accident last year, he was riding on a set of bald tires that Roger Sinclair wouldn't let Bump replace."

"Not now, Di," said Cookie.

"Roger Sinclair needs all his money for liquor and other women," said Diana.

Cookie looked embarrassed. "That's his business."

"Not if it affects the people who work for him."

Her cheeks were flaming and her voice was rising and she didn't seem to care that people were turning to stare at us. "It's my business, too, if there's no money for decent tires or a new valve for the presser or—"

"Okay, okay, we came to see the game." Cookie held up his hand.

The crowd roared as the first Volunteer batter punched a hit into short center, jumped on a donkey, and tried to kick him into speed. The donkey shambled toward first, stopping to nibble at the rider's knee. Cookie laughed so hard his chair shook.

I turned to Diana. She was wearing a light, flowery perfume. "I didn't mean to start a fight between you and—"

"You didn't start anything."

"Look, Diana"—just using her name gave me a thrill—"Roger Sinclair hired me, but he doesn't own me. I think you're right about conditions, I really do."

Cookie tapped my arm. "Come by the house after the game? We'll lift a few beers."

"I'd like that," I said.

The stench of cigar smoke drifted over, and a familiar voice boomed, "You get a real taste of Rumson Lake at a local shindig like this."

I pulled the peak of my cap down to my nose before I dared look over my shoulder to make sure the worst had happened. It had. Mr. Miller was posing in front of the bleachers, lecturing to Mrs. Miller and another couple. Someone yelled, "Down in front," and Mr. Miller gave him the cigar like a finger. But then he led the way to vacant seats nearby.

If the Millers saw me here Joanie would have a lot of explaining to do. Maybe it would be a good thing if her parents found out about her wonderful, terrible, beautiful, impossible affair before she got hurt. But that was none of my business. I'd made a commitment to her as a friend, and I couldn't let her get caught because of me. Damn!

"Got to go," I said to Diana.

Cookie grabbed my sleeve. "Coming back?"

"Not today. But I'd like a raincheck on your invitation."

"That's what they all say."

"No, really. Where do you live?"

"Out by Washington Road. Take the first—"

Mr. Miller boomed, "Let's hear it. 'We Want a Hit.' " He was standing up, playing cheerleader.

I slipped off the plank and scurried around to the back of the bleachers. Diana was saying something to Cookie. Probably telling him I was just a no-account summerboy anyway. I felt sorry for Cookie. And sorry for myself. I'd probably never have another chance at Diana.

13

I'd never seen my father so sick. The hernia operation had been a success, but he was allergic to the penicillin the idiot doctors gave him for the infection they let him catch in the hospital. The sharp bones of his cheeks and jaw seemed ready to poke through his papery skin. It took all his energy to smile at my laundry stories. I told him and Mom the stuff I thought they could handle— quick character sketches of Bump and Axel and Lolly and Ace, a little travelogue on the scenic routes, and a few of the milder off-color jokes from the diner. Nothing incriminating.

Dad drifted into sleep while I was talking, and Mom signaled me to follow her out of the room. "You've made him feel better already," she said in the corridor.

"Ought to sue these quacks," I said, loud enough to make a passing doctor flinch.

"Not so loud." She glanced around. "Fred Miller said the same thing. By the way, they'll be here in a little while, the Millers. You can get a ride back with them."

"Joanie coming too?"

"She had to work today."

I'll bet, I thought. "I'd rather take the bus home. So I can read." An hour of grilling by the Millers would break Nathan Hale.

In the hospital coffee shop Mom showed me the latest postcard from Michelle. A bunch of artsy-looking men and women were drinking wine at a sidewalk cafe in Paris called Aux Deux Magots. Michelle had written: "Wish vous were ici." I thought of Mignon and Marie. My face itched.

Mom said, "I sent a cable to the American Express office in Paris asking her to call us."

"You wrote Dad was sick?" When she shook her head, I said, "She won't call. She'll think you're just nagging her to come home. You should have said Dad was sick and wanted to see her."

"That would have been unnecessarily dramatic. Besides, I didn't want to worry her."

"You mean you didn't want to take the chance she'd still not call, knowing Dad was sick. You didn't want to risk the rejection."

"Please." She reached across the Formica tabletop to touch my face. "Don't psychoanalyze your mother until you're certified. And not even then." She stroked my cheek until her fingers touched a patch of rough new skin where the last scab had been. "Are you breaking out again?"

I jerked my head away. "Mom! We're in a restaurant!"

"I see a lot of marks on your face." She leaned forward until we were nose to nose. "Are you eating badly?"

"The berry-bush scratches, remember? I'm eating perfectly. Every food group at every meal, including yellow vegetables for breakfast. Cornflakes."

"I do not appreciate sarcasm," she said, but she was smiling.

We went back upstairs. Mr. and Mrs. Miller were sitting on Dad's bed. Mr. Miller was waving his dead cigar and entertaining Dad with a sound-effects version of the donkey baseball game, which had ended in a tie when the potential winning run stopped between third and home to water the basepath. Mr. Miller imitated Niagara Falls. That got a hacking chuckle out of Dad.

"Those people," said Mrs. Miller. "They're in their own little world. What's the name of that woman who goes to live with tribes?"

"Margaret Mead?" said my mother.

"She ought to do a book on Rumson Lake. Those people are as much natives as her headhunters."

I thought of Diana. "What do you mean?" My voice was a little sharper than I had planned. "They're people, just like you, they hope, they dream . . ." I trailed off, feeling foolish. Mrs. Miller looked confused.

Mr. Miller said, "Florence doesn't hope and dream. She just spends." He guffawed so hard Dad's bed shook. When he saw that nobody else was laughing, he said, "Well, we better let Marty get his rest." He patted Dad's cheek and shooed the rest of us out of the room. In the corridor, he said, "You call my lawyer yet, Lenore?"

Mom shook her head. "Marty's so much better now, and the doctors have been so concerned, very—"

"Slap 'em with a lawsuit, only thing they understand," said Mr. Miller. "Don't let 'em bury their mistakes."

While they talked, I slipped back into Dad's room. His eyes were closed, but there was more color in his face. I wanted to kiss him before I tiptoed out, but I thought it might embarrass him if he woke up. Or me. We stopped kissing when I was about six.

Mom walked us out of the hospital. She squeezed my arm. "Knowing you can take care of yourself has made all of this a lot easier, Bobby. Thanks for being you." She kissed me on a raw spot. "Now please go back with the Millers. For me. I don't want to have to worry about you getting home all right."

The Millers had driven their hardtop Cadillac into the city, and I sank into the plush backseat while Mr. Miller, chewing his dead cigar, tried to break every speed limit between Manhattan and Rumson Lake. I didn't get nervous until he took his eyes off the road to turn around and ask me, "How come you never told your folks about that crazy dive?"

"I was afraid Mom would slap you with a lawsuit." I couldn't help laughing. "I still might, you know."

"Your face is healed. There's no proof of damages." Mr. Miller wasn't laughing.

I felt very relaxed and comic. "I'll get an affidavit. And after David, I'll get Saul."

Mrs. Miller turned. "That's really very clever, Bob."

"That's not even original. I heard it on Groucho Marx." Mr. Miller sounded upset.

Mrs. Miller turned to say, "You know, Bobby, I didn't mean anything when I said Margaret Mead should study those people."

"I know. I'm sorry that I—"

"But don't you really, I mean really-really"—she blinked her furry eyelashes at me—"think they're different? Not bad different, of course, just . . . different."

"Not really. Given the same opportunities as—"

"Forget law," said Mr. Miller. "Be a headshrinker. Lotsa bucks and you can snooze while your patients tell you the story of their lives."

"Bob would make an excellent psychiatrist," said Mrs. Miller. She twisted around. "I think it's wonderful what you're doing for Andrew."

"Andrew?" As soon as I repeated the name, I knew I had made a mistake.

"The boy in Joanie's camp? The very fat boy?"

"Oh. That Andrew." Joanie was getting careless with her cover stories.

"Spending all that time at night with Joanie and Andrew. Telling him about when you were heavy." Her eyes narrowed. "You are spending a great deal of free time trying to help Andrew?"

"A boy like Andrew needs all the help he can get," I said.

"He certainly does." She turned away, letting me off the hook. Joanie was right. She didn't want to know. Not really-really.

"Forget Andrew," said Mr. Miller. "You get the goods on Roger Sinclair yet?"

"I hardly ever see him around. All I know is he won't let the foremen replace worn parts and he—"

"Be specific." Mr. Miller sounded alert and interested.

"One example, there's a valve on a pressing machine, it's some kind of safety valve for steam, and it's been leaking boiling water. If it ever blows off, it could scald somebody. But fixing it means shutting down the machine for at least a day and putting on a new valve, which is expensive."

"Anything else?"

"Lots of things on the trucks. Hoses, brakes, tires—"

"He's looking to sell out," said Mr. Miller.

"How can you tell?"

"If he wanted to keep the business, he'd be trying to build it up, improve, expand. But he's letting it go to hell and pocketing all the profits for himself."

"I lost you," I said. "If he's planning to sell, wouldn't he want the trucks and the machinery in good shape for a buyer?"

"Not bad for an English major." Mr. Miller turned to throw me a wink. He turned back in time to avoid a bus. "But you're wrong. Nobody's interested in those

trucks or machines. Automation's going to change everything soon. The big selling point is the grandfather
clauses."

"Grandfather clauses?"

"Towns make special deals with companies about
who can do business where. They go way back, that's
why they're called grandfather clauses. Lenape's got ex-
clusive laundry rights in the area. The routes are worth
a fortune. I can use this information."

"How?"

"It'll give me an edge. Anytime you know something
that someone doesn't know you know, you've got an edge.
Some free advice?"

"Sure." I was impressed at how he had created a
theory out of a few facts.

"Always play your cards close to the vest. Don't
let the competition know what you're thinking or what
you know. Keep your mouth shut till it's time to bite."

"Oh, Fred. What a thing to tell the boy."

"You remember this, Bobby. In business, in games,
in love, whatever, keep your mouth shut till it's time to
bite." He chuckled appreciatively at himself.

"If Roger Sinclair sold out," I asked, "what would
happen to the people who work there?"

Mr. Miller shrugged. "Who knows?"

"Could some of them lose their jobs?"

"That's business."

"It doesn't seem fair," I said.

"Roger the Dodger's the owner. They just work there."

"What if they got together and—"

"Those people?" Mr. Miller guffawed. "They think unions are un-American. I heard they let Sinclair run off a union organizer last year. They'd never get together enough to help themselves."

14

"This was Cookie's route," said Ace one day as we clattered toward the Lenape Inn in a wheezing Curbside. "I used to ride helper for him on heavy loads."

"He ever talk about Diana?" I asked.

"Never shut up. Di this, Di that, captain of the girls' basketball team, spittin' image of her dead mother, straight-A average. She should of been a boy, know what I mean?"

"No, what do you mean?"

"Here we go." He turned into the dim, cool corridor of giant firs that led to the Inn. "What good's all her brains and big ideas? She's stuck in zilchburg."

"If Cookie hadn't wracked up, she—"

"Nah, women like her are never satisfied. Here's another one, right here, this old bat counts the napkins ten times 'cause no guy's giving her what she really needs." As he pulled up behind the back door of the Inn's kitchen, the head housekeeper marched out, a grim expression on her face and a clipboard in her hand. Ace said, "Take a hike if you like. I'll be a while."

It was late in the afternoon, but I thought Joanie's day camp might still be in session, so I climbed up the path that led around to the front of the hotel. I hadn't talked to Joanie since the day of the donkey baseball game nearly a week ago. I hadn't talked to Diana since that day, either. At work, she turned her back on me or looked right through me. I'd tried to reach Joanie a few times, but she was always out when I called. Two women in my life and I wasn't even getting conversation.

I reached the crest of the hill and stopped to admire the layout. The Lenape Inn was the swankiest resort in the area. Golf course, indoor and outdoor pools, a nightclub. Below me, in a natural hollow, a man and a woman played tennis on one of the four tan clay courts.

They had strong, confident strokes. They didn't seem to be trying to get each other out, but to keep the ball in play. I felt like a peeping Tom as the ball moved back and forth between them, steady and low and deep. It was as if they were touching each other with the ball.

I thought I should leave, respect their privacy, but I was held by something familiar about the tennis players, the angles of their bodies, the way they held their heads, the sound and rhythms of their voices drifting up to me. I couldn't tune in their words.

Finally, laughing, the girl missed. I thought she might have missed on purpose so she could drop her racquet and rush into the man's arms. They kissed, a long, lingering kiss.

He spun her around. I could see Joanie's face very clearly, happy and flushed. Then the man's face.

Roger Sinclair.

I must have stood there a long time, stunned, because suddenly the court was empty, and a truck horn was honking impatiently. I stumbled down the hill.

"Where you been?" asked Ace, but before I could answer, the truck was moving and I had to jump in. He talked nonstop all the way back to the laundry, but I barely heard a word. Joanie and Roger Sinclair. I should have figured it out long ago. Some observer.

They must have met at the Millers' big party. That had been Roger Sinclair whom Joanie had been talking to in the driveway as I skulked past with my scraped face.

That day she had come into the laundry yard and provided me with the dramatic exit from the no-fight with Cliff—she must have driven in to catch a glimpse of Roger.

I remembered how nervous Roger had got when I had said, "I've found out some things," and how he had relaxed when I had told him it was about dangerous conditions in the laundry.

I wondered if he really wanted me to spy for him or if he was just playing me for laughs. I might never know. But it didn't take a secret agent to figure out why he was avoiding me now. He must know I was Joanie's friend, but he wasn't sure how much I knew about his affair.

Crazy, destructive, Joanie had described it. He calls me his single candle, she had said. Guess who was going to get burned.

15

The summer began to settle down and flatten out. My groove turned into a rut. Up early, out on routes that got less and less interesting, the same talk with the same guys, day after day after day. I got so plastered last night. Mantle and Snider and Mays. Joe D. was the one, boys. How'd you like to pound that into the ground? Mount up, let's go.

Nobody gave me a hard time, but nobody offered me any friendship, either. Our relationships ended when the working day was over. For a while I thought it was me, that none of the guys wanted to bother getting close to a summerboy who would soon be gone. Then I realized that they all went their separate ways after work, the married guys home to their families, Cliff to his mother, Ace to the girl he was seeing in Grantsville. Once in a while there was a softball game or a bunch of us went bowling, but that was just an extension of work, Cliff and Red commenting on the women, Jim and Ace talking baseball. I discovered that I'd rather be alone. Or at Spiro's, where the girls began to look better.

Weekends I went into the city to visit Dad, which would have put a crimp in my social life, if I had had one. He was getting well. He'd be home soon. So would Michelle. She was returning on the Queen Mary. Sometimes Mom asked about Joanie. I would say, "She's keeping herself busy."

Toward the end of July, Roger Sinclair was gone for a few days on a business trip. On a hunch, I called Joanie. Mrs. Miller told me that Joanie had quit her job to go to Boston for a week. Her college was running a special honors seminar for incoming sophomores. Mrs. Miller was vague—she said it had come up at the last minute and Joanie hadn't had time to tell them all the details.

It might have been my imagination, but I thought Roger Sinclair looked pretty smug when he returned from his "business trip." He certainly was tanned. I wondered if they had gone to Boston. Probably to Cape Cod. They lay on the beach in Provincetown and laughed about the demented greasers, drabs, harridans, cockeyed wenches, and hayseed bar brawlers sweating away their lives at the Lenape Laundry. And the summerboy who had been hired to give Roger a chuckle now and then.

A few days after Roger Sinclair returned, I was so late coming back on a run with Cliff that the laundry was deserted when I finished washing up and changing my clothes. I stepped out of the MEN's locker room into the dim, silent room. The abandoned machines looked like prehistoric monsters in the eerie light that leaked around the drawn shades and filtered through the dusty air. My nostrils stung from the bleach and soap powder.

How could anyone work in such a place? I tried to remember what it was like.

I heard voices.

"Di, honey, I've got a family to support. I'm thinking of them." It was Bump.

"He wouldn't dare fire you. He needs you too much."

"Who knows what he'll do?"

"Everybody sees what he's doing. He's bleeding this place dry. And we're the ones who suffer. There's a steam valve on the—"

"I know. Ol' Swede told me. Believe me, I got the same thing with half the trucks."

"Like the one that turned over on Daddy?"

"Di, please. That's ancient history."

"Not to me. I come home to it every night."

"Have a heart." I couldn't believe Bump was pleading. "What can I do?"

"You could be a leader. The drivers look up to you. You could tell them to stand up for better conditions. It's their lives. And if they did, the women would, too, and we could tell Sinclair that we'd all walk out if he didn't fix—"

"A strike?" Bump sounded shocked. "That's Commie stuff, that's—"

"You think I'm a Communist?"

"Course not, honey. Look, tell you what I'll do. I'll talk to the boys. I will."

"When?"

"Soon. You can't just hit 'em with something like

this. Got to ease into it. Little by little. Let 'em chew it over. Di? Where you going?"

I heard her quick, rapping steps fade away. Then I heard Bump curse, and his heavy, slower steps in the opposite direction.

My breath came out in a rush. I hadn't realized how long I'd been holding it. When I thought they were both gone, I started across the dark room toward the side entrance, trying to avoid jutting machinery. I heard harsh, dry sobs. Diana was leaning against the time clock. I had an overwhelming urge to put my arm around her, to comfort her.

"What are you sneaking around for?"

"No sneak." My tongue felt wooden. "Dark here."

"Go tell Mr. Sinclair what you heard. He's still in his office." She marched out to the yard.

I followed her. "I'll tell him anything you want, I really will. I think you're right. I really do. Let's talk about it. I'm on your side." The words just fell out of my mouth. "Can I see you after work?"

"It's after work. You've seen me."

"You know what I mean."

"I don't go out with summerboys." She picked up speed. I had to skip to keep up.

"Why not?"

"Because life is too short to waste a minute on people who are just passing through, people who use other people, then throw them away like Kleenex." She opened the door of an old Ford.

"I'm not like that. I'd really like to go out with you."

"Not interested." She got into the car and started the engine.

"What if I visited your father?"

She gave me a withering look. "You would use him to get to me?"

"That's not what I . . ." I tasted the fumes of her exhaust as she pulled away.

I wasn't thinking very clearly as I plunged back into the laundry. I had no idea what I wanted to say as I opened Roger Sinclair's frosted-glass door and stepped into his little office.

He looked up from a book. "Employees knock," he said coolly.

"Spies don't bother."

He cocked an eyebrow. "I hope this isn't another 'dangerous conditions' report."

"No. It's about you."

"I can hardly wait," he said in his usual sardonic tone. But he couldn't control the stiffening of the little muscles around his mouth or the twitching of his left eye.

I felt a little thrill of power. He was scared of me. Of what I might know. Of how I might use that knowledge. It would feel so good to let him know what I thought of him, rotten two-faced bastard, cheating on his wife, cheating on his employees, playing with Joanie. I could imagine him reeling helplessly under the onslaught of my fiery words.

And then what? Would anything I said right now make him fix the valve or overhaul the trucks? Probably not. Save it. Keep the edge. Keep your mouth shut till you're ready to bite.

"You're looking to sell the laundry."

I could almost feel the pent-up air whoosh out of his lungs. "What leads you to that conclusion?"

"You're not maintaining the machinery."

"It's simply good business," he said smoothly. "We're on the verge of incredible breakthroughs in technology. Within ten years people will be wearing plastic shirts and sleeping on paper sheets. The entire laundry industry will be revolutionized. It makes no sense, cost-wise, as they say, to put money into obsolete machines."

"What about people-wise? What about letting Cookie go after he wracked up?"

"He couldn't drive anymore. Don't worry about him. He gets workmen's compensation and Social Security. He can watch TV and drink beer all day." He smiled at me. "You're a nice boy, Bob, a little naive, but that comes with the age. I suggest you stop seeing so many movies."

"What?"

"Are you playing *Shane*? Riding in to save the sod-busters?" There was a nasty edge to his laughter. "They don't want you or need you. Didn't you learn any Emerson at college?" When I shook my head, he said, " 'Every hero becomes a bore at last.' Emerson said that. And

Sinclair says, 'Marks, you are boring me.' " He swiveled his chair to show me his back.

I slunk out of his office. The rat had my number. Had Joanie told him all about me, or was I just easy to figure out? I was a wedge. The simplest tool.

The walk home seemed endless. I had no energy. There was an Eldorado convertible in my driveway. Joanie was on the front steps. In the fading light, her face seemed narrower than usual, as if a giant finger and thumb had pinched it. Before I could ask her what was wrong, she said, "I need your help. I'm pregnant."

16

Under the living-room light she looked pale and tired. Her eyes were red rimmed. I asked, "You sure?"

"I'm sure. I'm never late. I'm regular as a clock." Her voice was without expression.

"I read that sometimes periods are delayed by emotional turmoil and—"

"Reading?" She dropped onto the love seat. "Got something to drink?"

"Root beer, orange juice, lemonade?"

"Scotch and water be fine." She lit up a cigarette. It was a Gauloise. "Easy on the water."

"You get a rabbit test?"

"I don't need one. I'm nauseous in the mornings. I go to the bathroom every ten minutes. My breasts tingle."

I found a dusty bottle of Scotch in the kitchen. My hand shook as I poured.

"What are you going to do?" I handed her the glass.

"I've got to get rid of it." She gulped half the Scotch and sighed. Just like Roger Sinclair.

"An abortion?" The word scared me. I'd heard too many stories in the dorms.

"I've tried everything else. Castor oil, hot baths, I even went horseback riding."

"What about the father?"

"That's irrelevant."

"Not according to my biology book."

"The father's not involved in this. He . . ." Her face got red and twisted. She took a deep breath and swallowed the rest of the Scotch. She stubbed out her cigarette and lit another. "He's got his own problems."

"He's pregnant, too?" It just slipped out. I didn't like the way I was acting, but I couldn't help it.

"Look, Bob, if you're going to be sarcastic—"

"Okay, okay. What about your parents?"

"They don't know anything."

"What about the money? It could cost five hundred dollars."

"I've got the money."

"Where'd you get it?"

"What are you, Martin Kane, Private Eye?"

A bell rang in my head. I'd used that line when Roger Sinclair called to ask me to spy for him. Of course, it could be a coincidence—it was one of the most popular shows on the air. But then maybe it wasn't a coincidence. Maybe Roger Sinclair repeated to Joanie everything I said to him. Maybe they laughed at me while they were lying real close.

Knock it off. Your friend is in serious trouble and you're acting like it's a plot to embarrass you. Grow up.

125

"Well," I said, trying to sound cheerful, "if we put our heads together I'm sure we'll come up with something. Two heads, at least."

She gave me a forced smile. "I knew I could count on you."

"First of all, let's review the possibilities." I tried to sound like Mr. Miller's version of a take-charge guy who wasn't afraid to reach for the brass ring. "Assuming this isn't a false alarm—you know, I've read about hysterical pregnancies where the woman swelled up even though—"

"I'm sure, Bob."

"Just wishful thinking. Okeydoke. You know, you could have the baby and give it up for adoption?"

She shook her head. "My father would die if he knew about this."

"You're going back to school in another month. Then comes wintertime, heavy clothes." I counted on my fingers. "You'd give birth around—"

"They'd kick me out of school. Bob, no, I've really thought about this. I don't want to have a baby."

"Okeydoke. That leaves—"

"Do you have to keep saying that?"

"Saying what?"

"Okeydoke. Where'd you pick that up?"

"In the laundry. The foreman, Bump—"

"The Neanderthal." She nodded.

"What do you mean, the Neanderthal?"

She bit her lower lip. "I, uh, guess you must

126

have called him that when you were telling me about—"

"I never called him that." The anger was rising again, and this time I didn't try to swallow it back. "At least Bump's no slimy fake who doesn't give a damn about anybody but himself, who cheats on his wife and turns his back on his girl friend and—"

"What's that supposed to mean?"

"C'mon, what kind of a tool you think I am? I know about you and Roger Sinclair."

She seemed to shrink into the corner of the love seat. She tucked her legs under her body and lowered her chin to her chest and hugged herself. I knew I should sit down next to her and put my arm around her and comfort her, but I felt too much rage. I wished I were a better person.

"It's not what you think," she whispered.

"Why the hell weren't you careful?"

"He hates to use anything. He says it's like wearing galoshes in the shower." She lit another cigarette. "I thought I knew what I was doing."

"He give you the money?" This time I couldn't say his name.

Joanie nodded.

"You're doing a lot better than some people who've had accidents with him. He treats his workers like dogs."

"You don't know him, Bob," she said very softly. "He's a very special person. No father and his mother was a cleaning lady. She put him through college.

"He won a fellowship to graduate school. He was

going to be a college professor. He was writing his thesis when a girl he was dating got pregnant. She was a fellow student. They weren't even in love."

She took a deep breath. She seemed to be holding back tears. I felt sorry for Joanie, swallowing Roger Sinclair's story. The tweedy version of my-wife-doesn't-understand-me-but-you-do. CLICHÉ!

"She wouldn't get an abortion, so he married her. He felt it was the only honorable thing to do. She made him move back to Rumson Lake with her, and her family made him work at the laundry. When her father died, he had to take over. He feels very trapped here."

She smiled. "I know this sounds crazy, but he reminds me of you, sometimes. He's so smart and gentle, he's funny, he's got this tough, smart-aleck facade, but underneath—"

"I get the general idea," I said. "So how come this special person isn't around in the clutch?"

She began to cry. I sat down next to her. "We'll take care of it."

She leaned against me. I just stroked her hair and let her cry it all out. It took a while.

Finally she said, "Do you know anybody?"

"I know Dr. Bushkin."

"Never." She shook her head. "If my father ever found out that—"

"You nuts? Why would Dr. Bushkin tell anybody? He's breaking the law. If he was caught he'd lose his license and go to jail."

"Oh, Bob," she moaned.

"Well, a couple of guys in the dorms took girls for abortions. I could call them. One of them went somewhere in Brooklyn, it was really dirty—"

She shuddered. "A girl at school had one. She started bleeding the next day—she nearly died."

"There's that famous doctor in Pennsylvania who gets away with it because he's the only one who'll go down into the mines. The local police leave him alone. But I really think Dr. Bushkin's our best bet."

"How could I face him?"

"You'd rather go to some stranger?"

"I don't know."

"He's careful. He's a good doctor. He's a nice guy. I'm sure he'd do it for you."

"Would you call him?"

I had to wait for my throat to open up again before I managed to say, "Okeydoke."

17

We didn't say much on the ride into the city. Joanie seemed very small, hunched into a corner of the front seat. I had never driven a Cadillac before, but under the circumstances it was no fun. We drove with the convertible top closed, despite the heat, as if we were in hiding.

Dr. Bushkin's office was on a quiet street in upper Manhattan. Just as I turned onto the block, a car pulled out of the parking spot across the street from the office. I pulled right in. "That's a good omen," I said. "Everything's going our way."

We were early, so we went into a nearby luncheonette. Joanie ordered tea with lemon. Mrs. Bushkin had instructed me over the phone to warn the patient against eating solid food on the day of the operation. I hadn't told Mrs. Bushkin who the patient would be. I just said I was calling for a friend. That seemed good enough for her. She was very businesslike—she said the patient had to arrive precisely at 6 P.M., bring $350 in cash, and tell no one else about the appointment.

I had a bacon-lettuce-and-tomato sandwich on rye toast. With mayo. I could have eaten more, but it didn't seem right to stuff my face while Joanie hardly touched her tea. I always got hungry when I was nervous.

The luncheonette was filling up with women, maybe a dozen of them, mostly big, husky women who seemed to know each other. A lot of them had big, blue handbags. I wondered if they all worked in the same place, if they were saleswomen who met here every day, like the Lenape drivers at the Rumson Diner. But they kept their voices low, and they looked serious.

"Bob?" Joanie's voice sounded muffled. "If anything happens, I want you to just leave."

I suddenly wanted another sandwich. Maybe two cheeseburgers. I ordered a glass of milk and changed the subject. "Does he know you're here today?"

"No. I'll tell him when it's over. He gets very nervous."

"Boss Cool?"

"You don't know that side of him, Bob. When we took our trip, I was swimming in the ocean, he lost sight of me for just one minute and he started—"

"Provincetown?"

"How did you know?"

"Just a guess."

"You know how you knew?" She grabbed my hand across the luncheonette table. "Because that's where you would have taken a girl you loved. The two of you are secret sharers, Bob. In another context, you would have been great friends."

I let that go by. I didn't want to argue with her

now, risk getting her upset. "You going to see him anymore?"

"He's very upset, he blames himself—"

"I wonder why?"

"Please, Bob. Not now."

"Sorry. Are you going to see him?"

"Not for a while. He wants to let things calm down. But I'm sure we'll be together again, somehow, somewhere." She glanced up at the clock over the counter. "It's almost six."

I swallowed my milk in two gulps.

As I paid the check at the cashier's desk near the door, I had the feeling that all the women were staring at us. Guilty conscience. That's why bank robbers are always giving themselves up, years after they've pulled the job and gotten away clean. They crack under the psychological pressure of always thinking everyone is looking at them, recognizing them from the Wanted posters in the post office. Paranoia.

Joanie set a determined pace back to Dr. Bushkin's street. She said, "Promise you'll leave if anything happens?"

"Everything's going to be fine." My stomach began to rise into my throat.

"I don't want you to get involved if something goes wrong. I don't want you to have a blot on your record. It could keep you out of medical school, or law school."

I had trouble keeping my voice steady. "Relax, kid.

132

Blots look good on a writer's record. Readers want to know you've been around."

"Thank you, Bob." Her first smile of the day.

We were in front of a street-level door with a white plaque in the window: ERNST BUSHKIN, M.D. The curtain behind the window moved. I imagined someone behind it, a lookout. I checked my watch. Six o'clock on the dot.

"Let's go in, please," said Joanie urgently, as if she was afraid that in another second she might change her mind.

I pushed the doorbell. The door opened while the bell was still ringing. Mrs. Bushkin nodded to me, then turned to Joanie. Her eyes widened in surprise. "Joanie!" Her eyes darted back to me.

I had an overwhelming urge to say, No, it's not me, I'm not the guy. Mrs. Bushkin said, "Come back in three hours. Precisely." She pulled Joanie into the office and slammed the door in my face.

I was glad I didn't have to go inside. And then ashamed for feeling glad. And then angry at myself for feeling ashamed for feeling glad.

I hurried away from the door. It could arouse suspicion if I was spotted hanging around in front of the office. I was already thinking like a criminal. I was a criminal. I had brought her here. That made me an accomplice.

I slipped into the stream of sweaty people coming

home from work, men with their jackets off and women with smeary makeup. I arranged my face into a weary mask, like theirs. No one could tell I was a hunted man.

C'mon, Bob. You are being unnecessarily dramatic. You're trying to enjoy this.

Several of the women from the luncheonette were standing on a corner, going over a list. Lights began to blink on in the tall apartment buildings along the street. People would be sitting down to supper soon. I wondered if I would ever be like one of these men on the street, hurrying from his job to his wife and kids.

I hoped not. I didn't want to be a nine-to-five man like my father. I wanted to have adventures. And then write about them.

I looked at my watch. I had two hours, thirty minutes, to kill.

Go to a movie. Go hide in the dark. Watch some make-believe guy have fake adventures. Hollywood heroes. No wonder you're such a meatball. You get all your ideas from movies. Roger Sinclair nailed you the very first day. Your secret sharer. That slimy crud.

I bought a copy of *The New Yorker* and went back to the luncheonette. Most of the tables were occupied by single people eating dinner while reading books and newspapers.

I ordered a deluxe burger with french fries and a chocolate malt and tried to read a short story about a young man who was nervous about spending the weekend with his grandmother. The story was so boring I knew there had to be hidden meanings, metaphors, symbols, clever ironies, but I couldn't find any. I concentrated so hard that by the time I finished the story, my glass and my plate were empty and I didn't remember tasting anything. I would have had dessert, but how could I eat chocolate pudding with a scoop of vanilla ice cream while Joanie was on the operating table?

I had one hour, forty-five minutes to kill.

I walked around the neighborhood. A pretty girl my age smiled at me and slowed down so I could pick her up. She was carrying *The New Yorker*, too. Probably going back to an empty apartment, I thought. What luck! Of all nights. Talk about clever ironies. I headed in the opposite direction.

Roger Sinclair should be here right now, pounding the pavement, worrying about what was going on behind Dr. Bushkin's door. But no, Joanie doesn't want to upset the fragile fellow, he's had such a hard life, college, graduate fellowships, a rich wife, understanding girl friends. I doubted that Joanie was the first.

There are guys like that, guys who waltz through life dropping their socks behind them for other people to pick up. Am I destined to be a picker-upper? I should have figured out Roger Sinclair that first day. The clues were all there. He was hiding from his family, boozing, whining about his unfinished thesis, ridiculing the people who worked for him.

If we get out of this with no problems, if Joanie's okay, I'm going to walk into Roger Sinclair's office tomor-

135

row and tag him one. On the button. And then walk out. No speeches, no explanation. If ever a guy deserved to be decked it's Roger Sinclair, taking advantage of every woman in his life. Probably doesn't even call his mother after she put him through college by washing floors. Treats his wife like dirt. Poor Joanie. And the women in the laundry, working under dangerous conditions so he can play around.

I had forty-five minutes to kill.

I decided to walk past Dr. Bushkin's office, just in case they had finished early and were waiting for me. The street was quiet. Two women were standing at the corner. I felt them looking at me from the corners of their eyes.

A raid.

The word ran through me like ice water. I was always reading in the paper about women cops making lightning raids on abortionists.

I was about to be caught in a dragnet.

I circled the block again. They nodded to each other as I passed, as if to say, That's the one.

I felt a hand on my shoulder. "Hello. Nice evening, isn't it?"

"I don't know what you're talking about." Hang tough, don't give them any information.

There were three of them, all smiling at me. One of them was holding out a piece of paper. An arrest warrant? "We're talking about the Answer and the Way. The only Hope. Have you thought about Forever?"

I glanced at the paper. It was a flier for a church meeting. I headed in the opposite direction.

I had a half hour to kill.

I thought about Diana. If I punched out Roger Sinclair, I'd be fired and I might never see her again.

If I never saw her again it would be too soon. I should have figured her out right away, too. Look at the way she treated me, never gave me a chance. Made fun of me. While I built her up in my mind as some combination of Eleanor Roosevelt, Joan of Arc, and Doris Day.

You can have the whole bundle of them. Roger Sinclair, Diana, Neanderthal Bump, Ace. I'm gonna wash that group right outa my hair. I'm not going to hit anybody. Us yellow belts never kill, we just quit. Go in tomorrow, collect my pay, and walk out that door. Forever. That's the answer and the way. And the only hope.

It was almost three hours. Precisely.

I was still pressing the button when Mrs. Bushkin opened the door. She was supporting Joanie, whose face was slack and papery white. I must have looked alarmed, because Joanie murmured, " 'M okay."

She stumbled into my arms. Mrs. Bushkin said, "Call us tomorrow." I thought she glared at me before she closed the door.

Joanie slept on the ride home. She didn't wake up until we were almost at Rumson Lake.

"How you feeling?"

"Kind of fuzzy, from the anesthesia, I think. And

crampy. Dr. Bushkin said that would last for a few days, like a bad period."

"Everything go all right?"

"He said it did. He was very nice. He didn't make me feel crummy. I told him you weren't the father."

"You didn't have to do that," I said. Gallantly, I guess. But I was glad. "Back to your house?"

"Take me to your house, let me rest for a while before I go home."

"It's getting late. Your parents—"

"They never worry when I'm out with you."

I couldn't see her face in the darkness, but I heard no irony or sarcasm or hidden meanings in her voice.

She slept for a few more hours in my house, and then I made her breakfast. She was very hungry. I had lost my appetite.

"We better get our stories straight," I said. "What did we do last night? See college friends? Help old Andrew over his weight problem?"

"Went to the city," she said, her mouth full of egg and English muffin. "Saw a movie."

"Which one?"

"Any one. They won't ask."

It was nearly dawn when I drove her home. I helped her out of the car and walked her to the front door.

"Here's looking at you, kid," I said. She kissed me on the cheek.

I felt good. Not at all tired. I bounced a little as I walked along the lake. Joanie was going to be all right.

Everything had worked out. What's so bad about being a picker-upper? Better than making messes, right? Shane was a picker-upper, cleaning up the mess the ranchers and the sodbusters made. Bogart in *Casablanca* and Holden in *Stalag 17* were picking up after the Nazis. You can't get much messier than that.

All those movies ended with the hero going off into the unknown, having solved the problems of others, his destiny still in question. Very symbolic. I might add that when I rewrite my freshman term paper for sophomore English.

The sun was rising over the lake. If I hurried, there would be just enough time to change my clothes, make my lunch, and get to work.

18

I got to the laundry in time to see the Fire Department volunteers carry out Lolly on a stretcher.

She was wrapped in a sheet. Her pink hair ribbon had come loose. It fluttered behind the stretcher like the tail of a kite. Diana walked beside the stretcher, holding Lolly's hand, stroking her forehead, murmuring to her.

The volunteers carried Lolly across the dock, set her down, and slid her into the rear of their ambulance. Except for the trailing pink ribbon, Lolly could have been a load of laundry. Diana climbed in with Lolly, doors slammed shut, and the ambulance pulled away, lights blinking, siren wailing.

The women stood silently in the yard, watching the lights diminish, then disappear. Some of them sobbed. Axel stood apart from them, frozen in a crouch, his hands balled into fists. "I tried to fix it best I could," he said.

"You did your best," said Bump. "It ain't your fault."

I asked one of the women, "Was it the valve?" When she nodded, I asked, "Is it bad?"

"She's seventy-four," snapped Diana's sidekick. "How can it be good?"

Roger Sinclair's MG careened into the yard. He jumped out, took one look at the crowd, and signaled Axel to follow him inside.

"Accidents happen," said Bump. "Let's get back to work, boys."

"Some accident," I muttered. "That valve's been leaking for a long time."

"You knew about it?" asked Cliff. He looked angry. "How come you didn't say nothing?"

"Where you been?" I said. "Ol' Swede kept fixing it because Sinclair wouldn't buy a new one."

"Okeydoke," said Bump, "let's get rolling. Nothing stops the Lenape Laundry." He threw me a shut-up look. I wondered if he was afraid the drivers would start thinking about the brakes and the hoses and the tires he couldn't replace. "Talk on your own time, we've got work to do."

At the diner, Cliff said, "We ought to do something."

"What's bugging you?" asked Jim.

"God only gives us one body," said Cliff.

"He only gave you half a brain," said Ace.

Cliff seemed too deep in thought to hear the crack and no one laughed. A waitress came over for our orders. "Whatsa matter, fellas?"

"There was an accident," said Red. "You know Lolly Kraus?"

"Eddie Polk's grandma?" She looked concerned. "What happened?"

"Got scalded," said Red. "And she might of broke something when she fell down."

"Maybe her hip," said Cliff. "Like my grandma. Old folks break their hips, and that's it. Never walk again."

"Like Cookie," I said.

"Why you trying to get everybody stirred up?" asked Jim.

"Whose side are you on?" I asked.

"No sides—we all work here," said Jim. "You know so much about it, why was she standing right under the valve if she knew it was bad?"

"Where was she supposed to stand?" I asked. "You think Axel would let her fold outside?"

"I got a question for you, Jim," said Cliff. "You ever tell Bump you won't take out Number Six till he fixes the suspension?"

"That'd be asking for a pink slip."

"See?" Cliff looked around triumphantly. "She didn't have no choice."

"You must of burned out your brain with all that thinking," said Ace.

"Cliffie's got something there," said Red. "Could be one of us next."

We worked at half speed through the morning. With the main presser out of action, less laundry came out of the plant and we rolled with short loads. We didn't dawdle on the road, either—we got back as soon as we could to find out what was happening. Axel returned from visiting Lolly at the hospital with a preliminary report: She had second-degree burns and bruised ribs, but nothing was broken, and unless she developed a secondary infection, she'd be all right in a couple of weeks. We all cheered, but I thought about my father, twenty-five years younger than Lolly, getting sicker in the hospital.

"That woman is one tough bird," said Axel. "When she saw me, she made Diana fix her hair ribbons."

"Di always wanted to be a nurse," said Bump. "Remember how she took over when Cookie wracked?"

"We were just talking about that," said Cliff. "Two big accidents in two years."

"One thing's got nothing to do with another," said Bump.

"Maybe," said Cliff. "Ol' Swede couldn't put in a new valve and you couldn't do nothing about Cookie's bald tires."

"Suddenly you got so much to say," growled Bump. "You better get back to work or you can start saying it someplace else."

Diana returned during lunch hour, her face hard and her eyes feverish. She tacked up a sheet of paper above the time clock and one on the loading-dock door. We rushed over to read them. They were identical, neatly typed on hospital stationery. They read:

143

Bump and Axel tore the papers down before Roger
Sinclair got back from his usual long lunch, but by that
time everyone had read them. The air seemed to crackle
with nervous energy as we stood in a circle on the dock.

"Chick flipped her lid," said Ace.

"She's got balls, you got to give her that," said Red.

"I always gave her that," snickered Ace.

"She's right," I said. "Conditions stink."

"You don't like it," said Jim, "go back to college."

"This ain't the way to make changes," said Red.
"Just get Sinclair riled up. Make things worse. Got to
get Bump to talk to Sinclair."

"Be old as Lolly by then," said Cliff.

"Don't look now," said Ace.

Diana was marching toward us, another sheet of
paper in her hand. Bump hustled across the dock to head
her off. "Give us a break, honey, we know how you feel,
but —"

"Forget how I feel. It's all our arms and legs and
lives on the line here." She held out the paper. "Sign
it, Bump. Show your men you care about them."

144

"I . . . I can't." His little eyes sank deeper into his fat face. "I'm management."

"If you were really management, you'd be able to do something for us. Face it, you're just a worker like us." She whirled on Jim and Red. "How about you?"

Jim looked down at his shoes, and Red said, "Who's gonna take care of my wife and kids if I get canned?"

"Who's going to take care of them if a truck rolls over on you?"

Red shook his head and turned away.

"Ace?" She held out the petition toward him. "You're always talking so tough."

"I got my name on enough lists." He grinned and winked at me.

Cliff pointed to the paper. "How many names you got so far?"

"Three, including mine. But if you drivers sign, I'll be able to go back Inside and get more names from the women."

"I'll sign it," I said.

She ignored me. "Don't you understand? What happened to Lolly, what happened to my dad, could happen to any one of you. You've got to stand up for yourselves."

"Maybe this ain't the best way to do it, Di," said Bump. "Everybody's all upset now. Let's wait till we calm down. Think more clearly."

145

"I said I'd sign it." I took the petition out of her hand. Her name, as big as John Hancock's, came first, then two names so sloppily scrawled they were illegible. Purposely, I figured.

I signed *Robert A. Marks* very clearly, and handed back the paper. She said: "If he can do it, what about the rest of you?"

"He's just a summerboy," said Jim. "He's got nothing to lose."

Axel came out on the dock. He beckoned to Diana. "Let's go."

"As soon as I give this to Mr. Sinclair."

"You can't do that." He lunged for the paper but Diana jerked it away. Bump stepped between them. Axel said, "I can't let her do it, Bump. How does it look for me, I can't control my girls?"

Diana said, "How does it look, you can't keep them from getting hurt?"

"Just don't touch her, Axel," said Bump.

"She goes in there, that's insubordination," said Axel. "Right, Bump?"

Bump nodded. "Di, what's the point? You only got four names."

"I've got to do something," she said. "I can't do nothing."

"You go in there," said Axel, "and I fire you. Right, Bump?"

Bump looked miserable. "I can't help you this time, Di. Rules are rules."

I said, "I'll take the petition in." I snatched it out of her hand.

"Don't mess yourself up for her," said Jim.

"This is not for her," I said. "This is for me."

Jim hollered something else, but I was already moving into the soapy mist.

I kicked open the frosted-glass door.

"You better read this." I dropped the paper on Roger Sinclair's desk.

He read it quickly, smiling and nodding. "A real declaration of independence this, signed by three hysterical harpies and one sunshine hero."

"There's an old woman in the hospital because of you, and a man paralyzed for life."

"Don't push me, Marks. This is real life, not the movies." He tore the petition into a dozen scraps and dropped them into my hand. "Go tell those people to start earning their pay before I replace them with people who will."

"I'm going out to tell them to stop working until you promise to meet with a committee."

"Wait a minute." He stood up. He was smiling. Somehow, the crooked teeth made him seem vulnerable, friendly. "Look, I felt the same way myself when I first got here. I wanted to help these people. But you can't. They're different from you and me. They're narrow, suspicious of outsiders."

"That gives you the right to exploit them? To make them work under dangerous conditions?"

147

"Aren't we self-righteous and satisfied." His smile turned into a sneery grin. "You must have helped a lot of old ladies across the street today."

I answered slowly, in a monotone. "No, but yesterday I drove a young lady into the city."

His eyes narrowed. "So?"

"She had an accident, too. Because of you."

"What are you talking about?"

I enunciated my words very carefully. "Joanie Miller had an abortion yesterday."

He took it like a shot in the mouth. His head jerked back, his body quivered, his face turned gray. He sat down.

For at least a minute, the only sound in the little office was Roger Sinclair's breathing, rapid, shallow, raspy.

I felt triumphant. A verbal knockout punch. Maybe I wasn't such a simp after all.

Finally, he looked up at me. His face was expressionless. His voice was chilly. "You're fired, Marks."

"Huh?"

"If you're not off the laundry grounds in five minutes I'm calling the police to arrest you for trespassing."

"You can't call the police. A married man, cheating on his wife."

The sneery grin was back. "Do I detect a hint of blackmail? Wise up, Marks. You're the criminal here. Accessory to an abortion. There's no way you can tell anyone, the police, my wife, about Joanie and me without implicating yourself in a felony. Now clear out. You've got four minutes."

I had a sudden urge to grab him by his striped tie and smash his crooked teeth down his throat. I clenched my fist and picked my spot. Then I thought, What if he's right about that accessory-to-a-felony business? And if anything gets out, Joanie would be hurt the most. I shoved my hands in my pockets to control myself.

My voice sounded wavery, childish. "You know what you are? A pimp. That's what you are."

"Three minutes." He put his hand on his telephone. I noticed that his hand was trembling. But my whole body was shaking.

"A pimp. You live off women. Your wife and Joanie and Lolly and all the other women who work here."

His face was twisted. "Time's up, Marks." He lifted the receiver and began to dial.

I walked out of his office, through the soap fog, to the dock. Diana was standing exactly where I had left her. "He told you to mind your own business, didn't he?" she said. "He sent you packing."

I kept walking.

19

I walked to the end of the dock, stepped up on a cart of clean laundry, and vaulted to the top of a half-loaded truck. My work shoes clanged on the metal roof.

The women in the yard looked up.

"See this?" I shouted. I tossed the scraps of the petition into the air. They floated down like paper snow. "That's what Roger Sinclair thinks of you."

Every face was pointed at me. Every eye watching, every ear cocked. I had never felt such power.

"Roger Sinclair put Cookie in a wheelchair. He put Lolly in the hospital. Who's next?"

Open-mouthed silence. I could have heard a soap bubble pop.

Roger Sinclair appeared in the doorway of the dock. He shouted: "He's only a summerboy, he'll say anything. He's got nothing to lose."

"I'm only a summerboy. I've got nothing to gain."

"Get him down from there, Bump," screamed Roger Sinclair. "Or you can follow him right out of here."

Bump started toward me. His head was down and he wasn't moving very fast, and I could see his heart wasn't in it. I thought he looked relieved when Cliff stepped in front of him, his Herculean arms crossed on his massive chest. Bump turned to Roger Sinclair and shrugged.

Cliff shouted, "Keep talkin', summerboy."

"We've got to stand together, all of us. Foreman, folder, Inside, Outside, city boy, all-year-rounder, driver, man, woman, it doesn't matter."

"Axel! Get inside and call the police!"

It seemed as though Axel waited until Red and Jim could grab his arms. He pretended to struggle.

"Back to work," screamed Roger Sinclair. His face was red, he was waving his arms wildly. "Anybody who isn't back to work in one minute is fired."

Diana climbed up beside me on the truck roof. She shouted: "He can't fire all of us or he won't have a laundry. If we stick together we'll be all right. He'll have to make this place safe for us."

Roger Sinclair jumped off the side of the dock and sprinted toward his car. Women jumped out of his way, a white sea parting.

Diana shouted, "The drivers stuck their necks out. What about us?"

Like one great white amoeba, the women flowed across the yard and surrounded the MG. They sat on it, they covered it with their bodies.

"Everybody's together, Sinclair," I shouted. "They won't go back to work unless you promise to overhaul all the trucks, replace the presser valve, and meet with a committee, once a month."

"Is that summerboy talking for all of you?"

There was a moment of silence, then Cliff yelled, "He's talkin' for me," and drivers and women started shouting and I thought even Bump and Axel were nodding their heads. I had tears in my eyes.

Roger Sinclair stood in the middle of the yard, a patch of brown cord in a sea of white. His shoulders were slumped. He was defeated.

Suddenly he looked up. "Okay. On one condition." He pointed at me. "That sonuvabitch goes. Right now!"

I could tell he meant business. So could the others. They looked at each other and at me and down at their shoes. They muttered and shook their heads.

Diana touched my arm. She said softly, "You do whatever you think is right."

I looked at her. She was smiling at me. I said, "I'd just be in the way now."

Then I shouted down to Sinclair, "You got yourself a deal."

They were all cheering and hugging each other and slapping backs, so nobody seemed to notice that I nearly fell on my face jumping from the truck roof to the dock. So it wasn't an all-time move. Ace, who was closest, was busy shaking hands with Cliff. There's a metaphor. Cliff a hero and Ace a zero. Never would have figured it. Somebody could write a thesis on that.

I dropped down from the dock to the yard. I was still in my uniform. Sinclair could have the old dungarees and the ratty college T-shirt I'd left in my locker. As if he needed something to remember me by. I'd keep my cap and the Indian-head whites for a souvenir.

At the gate, I turned to give anyone who was looking a farewell wave, but no one was looking. Roger Sinclair was talking to Bump and Axel and Diana. Jim and Red and Ace and Cliff were each holding court with a cluster of women. Telling how they won the great laundry war. My hero.

If this was the movies, I would have been able to give a little speech, like Holden in *Stalag 17.* "If I ever run into any of you bums on a street corner, just let's pretend we never met before."

No speech. I just gave a little wave in case someone was looking and headed home. I imagined the words THE END superimposed on my back, just under the Indian head.